The Legend of SNOW *and* LITTLE ROSE

D.C. TOWNSEND

ISBN 978-1-957776-03-3 (Paper Back)
ISBN 978-1-957776-04-0 (Hard Back)

GroveHouse Press LLC 340 S Lemon Ave #3529
Walnut, CA 91789 United States

www.grovehousepress.com

Printed in the United States of America

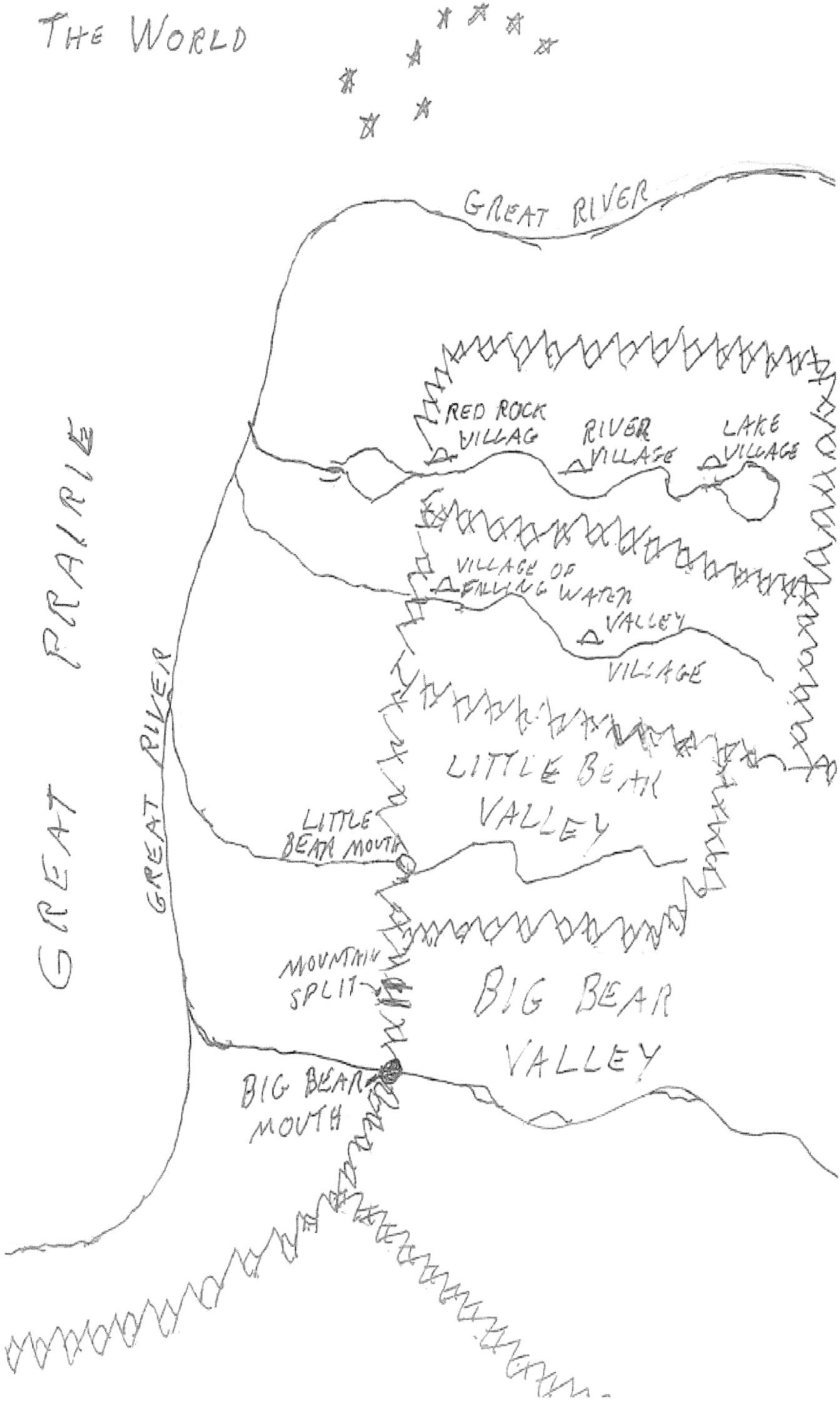
THE WORLD
GREAT RIVER
RED ROCK VILLAG
RIVER VILLAGE
LAKE VILLAGE
VILLAGE OF FALLING WATER
VALLEY VILLAGE
GREAT PRAIRIE
GREAT RIVER
LITTLE BEAR VALLEY
LITTLE BEAR MOUTH
MOUNTAIN SPLIT
BIG BEAR VALLEY
BIG BEAR MOUTH

CHAPTER 1

The mountains, some with snow-white tops in midsummer fed small streams that weaved through the hills to the river that flowed down the valley. This was a rich land, with an abundance of flora and fauna. In the valley along the river lived a peaceful people. For generations they thrived, living in peace and harmony with their world. This is one of their legends.

There was a blizzard blowing. In their lodge was Soaring Raven; his wife, Spring Flower; a midwife, a stately woman in her early fifties; and the midwife's apprentice, a woman in her middle twenties. Spring Flower was giving birth.

Midwives were highly respected members of the community. All midwives had at least one apprentice, as well as an apprentice assisting. It was necessary that a midwife's knowledge be passed down from one generation to the next. It was very important that no village be left without a midwife.

Soaring Raven set upon the laid-out hides with his legs spread out in front of him. Spring Flower lay between his legs with her head on his stomach. They were grasping each other's hands. Spring Flower alternated between gasps of air and pushing, with moans and grunts, all at the coaching of the midwife.

Finally, after one very loud groan, the midwife tied off and cut the umbilical cord. She held up an infant, pronouncing, "A boy."

Holding him up by the feet, she gave the infant a firm pat on his back. The expected scream did not come but a sputter. The midwife held out her hand to be handed a dampened cloth by her apprentice. The midwife promptly wiped the infant's mouth then his chest. The blizzard blowing outside with the heavy breathing of both the mother and father added to the drama. The midwife placed her ear against the infant's chest, occasionally moving her ear about. The parents looked on with great concern.

Finally, the midwife pronounced, "Good lungs and a strong heart." A sigh of relief came from both parents.

The mother asked the midwife, "Is it a sign that he did not cry?" This was Spring Flower's fourth birth; she knew what to expect.

The midwife replied, "Maybe his just does not want to cry. Some babies cry a lot. Some not so much." The midwife continued cleaning up the newborn while examining every bit of him, even counting fingers and toes. Her apprentice tended to the mother and afterbirth. The midwife finally placed the newborn upon the mother's bosom, pronouncing, "A beautiful, healthy boy." The infant's body was covered with a small rabbit fur blanket, fur side in for warmth, hide side out for protection from drafts.

Spring Flower pointed to the flap of their lodge, telling Soaring Raven, "Look outside for a sign?" It was the tribe's tradition upon a birth that the father looks outside for a sign from the great spirits; a sign for the name of their newborn child.

He did what he was told, sticking his head through the flap looking around. Shortly, he pulled his head in, looked at his wife, saying, "Snow."

With a look of bewilderment, Spring Flower said, "That would be a dumb name. Go out and look."

Soaring Raven donned his winter parka, leaving the lodge. He was gone several minutes. Upon his return, with a look of frustration, he raised his hands, saying, "Big Snow."

Spring Flower now requested that he open the flap wide so she could look. He did as requested. Snow blew into the lodge. Spring Flower sat up, craning her neck to see.

The midwife ordered, "Close that flap before the baby gets a chill." Soaring Raven did as he was told.

The parents looked at each other. After a brief pause, both of them said, as if in the same breath, "Snow."

The midwife repeated. "Snow." As did the apprentice. It was getting dark the midwife left. She left her able apprentice to watch over the mother and newborn till morning. Soaring Raven escorted her back to her lodge, only a few lodges away. He returned with their son, Running Deer, to introduce him to his new brother. Running Deer, there firstborn, was now eight years old. They had two daughters that were taken from them by the fever that plagued their village two winters ago. The apprentice tended to the needs of the mother and child. She coaxed the mother to sip water, giving her some broth as well as some meal with small pieces of fresh fish in it. Some of the women of the village had prepared these especially for Spring Flower when she went into labor. All the villagers worked together for the well-being of all. Sloth and selfishness were not tolerated in this village. The village had a strict code of behavior and morality; repeated infractions would bring banishment ordered by the council, although none remember anyone being banished. Most all problems or disputes were handled by the chief in private. All the chief's decisions could be challenged in council; nobody had ever challenged his decision.

The morning came, the snow had stopped, the sun was rising over the mountains to the southeast. The mother and baby were doing well. It was now time for Soaring Raven to present Snow to the village. The sky was clear, although the air was cold. An unofficial duty of a midwife was to spread the word that a birth announcement was to be made, though she never revealed the name or gender, which was reserved for the father. Soaring Raven stood out in front of his lodge. It was not long before many of the villagers gathered around. All were waiting for the chief and shaman. Upon their arrival, Soaring Raven retrieved the newborn from the lodge. He unwrapped the infant from the fur blanket and held the naked newborn high for all to see. Snow gave no sign of protest against the cold air. Soaring Raven then announced, "My son, Snow." He then quickly rewrapped his son.

The chief then took the precious bundle and held it up, saying, "All, welcome the newest member of our village, Snow."

The gathered villagers all said, "Snow."

Snow was now an accepted member of the village. The ceremony over, Snow was returned to his mother as the villagers went their way.

Some in the village wondered about Snow's odd name and his apparent oblivion to the cold air. None the matter, he was part of the village. All would share in the responsibility for his well-being. So was the start of a legend-to-be.

Snow's early years were mostly normal. He learned to crawl, talk, and walk at the appropriate ages. The mother, father, and others noticed that he was a little different than the other children. Totally different from what his brother was at a similar age. Snow almost never cried; where Running Deer threw crying tantrums. He was very shy and never demanding; whereas his brother was very outgoing and at times demanded attention. Snow was very curious about everything about him. He never seemed to get bored; he would watch and listen to birds or an insect for long periods of time. At about four, he would accompany his mother out into the woods to gather greens, herbs, roots, or firewood. He always insisted that he would help. No matter what it was, he would watch his mother then copy what she did. He learned very quickly by watching. When bringing in firewood, he would drag in a limb that his mom thought was too big for him to handle. She got tired of telling him, "A smaller one." So she would let him struggle. He was persistent and somehow would manage.

Once, a group of women were preparing food. Snow watched a woman grind grain between two rocks. After she was done, Snow put a handful of grain in the center then proceeded to work the top stone back and forth. All the women stopped what they were doing and watched this six-year-old boy grind grain. A couple of the women complimented that he was doing as good a job as they could do. The other women were always telling Spring Flower what a wonderful son she had. It was usually followed by a combination of the following, polite, always minds, is so helpful, never gets in the way, never gets in trouble, always listens, or does not talk much.

Snow always minded. Except he had a habit of wandering off. His curiosity was unrelenting. He would follow the sound of a bird into the woods or be found leaning over the riverbank, watching bugs skimming over the water. Snow learned to swim early. He wandered off, and his mother looked for him in a panic. She found him in a still area of the river, happily paddling around.

Spring Flower had her hands full. Her oldest, Running Deer, was rebellious and often got in trouble. Snow was always wandering off but was so agreeable that it was hard to punish him. After Snow, Spring Flower had two daughters, Yellow Bird and Autumn Leaves. By the time Snow was seven, Snow and his mom had come to an understanding. He did not wander too far, and his mom would leave him alone. His mom was busy with his sisters and older brother.

Snow rarely played with the other children. He preferred to watch the adults work. Then he would imitate them, becoming a helper. At eight he started to fish, often by himself. He was a successful fisherman. He often brought fish to the camp. By ten he was accomplished at building a lodge. Lodge building was mainly women's work, but the women did not protest his help. He worked well with others. He was cheerful and coconscious. By eleven he was known to make quality arrows and spearheads. By twelve he had made his own bow, arrows, and spears. Snow was going hunting with his father and his father's hunting partners. Quickly, Snow was accepted as a good hunter. He was patient and stealthy.

Red Hawk and Big Badger were slightly older than Snow. Occasionally, they went fishing together. The last time they want fishing together, Red Hawk and Big Badger ran up and down the riverbank, throwing their fishing spears at the fish as the fish swam away. On the opposite bank, Snow sat still on a log with the tip of his spear in the water, patiently waiting for the fish to come by.

Big Badger said, "Look at Snow. He is lazy, waiting for a fish to impale himself on his spear."

Red Hawk replied, "As ugly as Snow is, he probably is trying to scare the fish to death."

Snow answered, "I am going up the river. You two are making too much noise."

Big Badger responded, "Red Hawk cannot keep his mouth shut. He talks all the time."

Red Hawk immediately charged Big Bader. The two of them went in the water wrestling. Snow picked up his stringer of fish and headed upstream.

Late that afternoon, Red Hawk and Big Badger returned to the village, proudly showing off the six medium-sized fish that they had speared. Snow arrived with a stringer of many fish, some large, so many fish he had difficulty carrying them. The Chief had watched the boys return.

The chief said, “Snow, you are a good fisherman. The entire village will eat fresh fish tonight.” Then the chief gave a disapproving look at his son and Big Badger.

Red Hawk and Big Badger became Snow’s hunting partners. They accepted Snow to hunt with them because of his skills. He often would be the one to bag their quarry. He would let them take the credit. Red Hawk and Big Badger wanted to impress everyone, especially the eligible young girls, with their manly powers. They would strut and display whenever they got the opportunity. Before the village fires, they would paint their faces then dance with enthusiasm, declaring themselves fearless. Snow was content to just watch, not desiring to be brave and fearless. Red Hawk and Big Badger enjoyed ridiculing Snow, trying to goad him into a fight. Often it was “Snow is a dumb name,” “Snow likes to do women’s work,” “Snow is weak of mind and body,” “Snow is really a girl,” or other creative insults. No matter how hard they tried, they could not goad Snow into playing their macho games. Snow had no ambition or desire to be brave or macho, playing their games.

On one occasion, Red Hawk and Big Badger dared Snow into listening with them at the men’s lodge meeting. They got caught. They spent the night with their hands and feet bound, awaiting punishment in the morning. Their feet were unbound and led to the river. It was spring. The river water ran cold and deep.

The chief said, “You think that you are old, strong, and brave enough to be part of council? Let us all see what you have.”

The shaman smeared gray goop on their ears; then they were sent out into the river to stand in the water up to their waist while the whole village watched. All three of them stood bravely in the cold water, wanting to prove themselves. It started slowly. Their ears became warm; then their ears became hot. Their ears began to burn. The water was cold. Eventually, it felt like their ears were on fire. It became unbearable. Red Hawk, the chief's son, was the first to break. He screamed, diving into the cold water. He was soon followed by Big Badger. Snow closed his eyes and clenched his teeth tight. He could feel the tears running down his cheeks, but he stood strong; he knew his mother and father were watching. After a while, Snow could not feel his ears. He was sure his ears were gone, though he could still hear the water rippling about his waist. Snow's legs were numb. He felt himself wobbling. A hand grabbed his arm.

He heard his father's voice. "Come, son, you have had enough."

Snow opened his eyes as he was helped by his father to the riverbank. There, sitting on the bank, was his two comrades. They still had ears. Their hands were still bound. Upon reaching the shore, the chief unbound Snow's hands.

The shaman came to Snow with laughter in his voice. "By evening your ears will grow back."

As Snow and his father walked back to their lodge, his father said, "I am mad at you and proud of you at the same time. You broke the rules; then you took your punishment standing strong. We will never talk of this again."

Snow started to hunt by himself. He would sit waiting on a game trail. With patience, he would often be rewarded. He started to have a persistent pest. Little Rose, a skinny girl who was a year younger than he was started to follow him around. He would be sitting out in the woods and be tickled on the back of the neck. It would be Little Rose behind him with a small stick. How she could sneak up behind him, he did not know. Snow wanted to wrap his hands around her neck. She managed to bring ire into Snow's heart where the boys could not. After a couple times chasing her through the woods, having her elude him, he started to ignore her. She was so quiet and allusive she did not hamper his hunting. At least she was quiet and did not want to talk a lot, like most girls. Eventually, she would help him field dress his game then help carry it back to camp. Eventually, when Snow went into the woods, he knew she was nearby. On occasion, she would give a little sparrow whistle, warning Snow that there was game nearby. Often, if he moved extra slow and quiet he could get a shot. The other girls her age were working with the women, doing women's work. They were interested in attracting the boys, showing them how good of a wife they would make. The boys would act macho and tough, pretending to ignore the girls while they would parade in front of them.

Snow found himself looking at White Dove. Her breasts were becoming full and her hips well-rounded. She always had a nice smile. She would often look at Snow, smile, then look down like she was shy. On a couple occasions Snow tried to sit next to her at the campfire. The other boys seemed to always find a way to get between White Dove and him. Without a bear hide to present to a girl and being a member of the council, there would be no bonding.

One nice late-winter day Snow had managed to bag four turkeys. On his way back to the village as he passed by the crazy woman's small lodge he accidently dropped one of the turkeys and kept going. Little Rose stopped him, asking Snow what he was doing. He explained to her that when he was lucky in hunting or fishing he would try to share.

She asked, "Why do you not just give it to her?"

Snow said, "She is crazy, but she still has her pride. I will not shame her into accepting charity."

Little Rose asked, "Why do you do this?"

Snow replied, "My mother tells me to not forget her. She was once a strong woman who escaped from the evil Redface."

Little Rose asked, "Nobody talks of her. Can you tell me why she is crazy?"

Snow answered, "I can only tell you what my grandmother told me before she died. As a young girl, she was captured from another tribe by the Redface. They beat her and treated her badly. When she was a teenage girl, a Redface chief beat her, trying to have his way with her. She stabbed the chief with a knife then ran away. She went over the mountains, founding our village. She was sick and weak. She was taken in by a good man and his family. After she got better, many of our people got sick with a fever. All the family that took her in died from the fever. She blamed herself and went crazy. Now she lives at the edge of the village, finding her own food and eating our scraps. Nobody bothers her. She has been touched by the spirits."

It was spring. Snow knew that it was time for Red Hawk and Big Badger to be sent off to prove themselves. He had seen them making and practicing with large spears. Snow had seen his older brother go through the ritual a few years ago. He had not yet return, so his name could not be said until he returned.

After a council meeting, Snow's father came to him telling him, "It had been decided. Tomorrow, I will help you prepare for manhood." Snow thought he would have one more year before he would have to leave as a boy, and if he was successful, return a man.

Snow had already made two large spearheads. Last year, he found two flints that looked exactly right. Instead of breaking them up to make arrowheads, he made large spearheads. In the morning, Snow asked his father why he was not given another year to become stronger.

Soaring Raven explained, "The shaman said he had a vision that evil was coming. The tribe will need every man. He said to 'Send Snow to become a man. He will be needed.' He said we need to prepare to fight an old enemy."

Snow and his father went partway up the mountain to a stand of young birch trees. There they selected two straight trees of the right size that had only small limbs making small knots. These were cut to make two spears. They would be stripped of their bark and scraped, then the wood would be cured over a fire. These would make strong and stiff spear shanks. Snow's spearheads were carefully fitted to the spear shanks, making two weapons suitable to kill a bear. As soon as he was prepared, he would leave.

Soaring Raven gave Snow advice. "Do not go high where the large brown bears live. Kill a smaller bear. It is better to return with a small bear than be in a bear's stomach."

Snow questioned, "Father, you have a large bear that you and mother sleep on."

The father said, "I was lucky. He was a large black bear. He impaled himself on my spear. Up in the high country, the bears are brown. They grow to be giants. The bear that I speared would be food for a giant brown bear."

Snow said, "I have heard stories of great warriors killing a giant brown bear."

The father replied, "Yes, they are stories, not facts. You are my second son. I am still waiting for my first son to return to me. I want you to return to me."

Snow's father explained and showed Snow how to hold and use his spears.

Snow father told him, "You cannot kill a bear by stabbing him. You must lay your spear down than get the bear to charge you. When it is just right, you raise your spear, making sure the spear hilt is well anchored, let the bear impale himself. Even though the bear is running into your spear, his claws and mouth can still rip you to shreds. Some say to stand your ground, making sure your spear does its job. Others say to jump out of the way after the bear makes contact. In the council lodge, that is often a discussion that has never been resolved."

"Father, what did you do?"

"I do not know. I planned to stand my ground. It happened so fast; afterward I found myself lying on the ground in a daze.

"Father, what do you recommend?"

"Make sure your spearhead hits the bear solidly in his chest. The spear hilt is well anchored. After that, it is up to the great spirits."

Red Hawk had departed, going east toward the sunrise. Snow had accompanied Big Badger for a short distance as he went west, the direction of the setting sun. They talked, departing as friends. No wishes were made which might bring bad luck. As Snow was returning to the village, he was thinking which direction he would go. In a couple of days, he would be on his journey, hopefully to manhood.

As Snow walked, he thought of the story told at the bonfire of a time many generations ago when his people first came to their valley. The story was that at that time, there were many black bears in the valley that took the people's food, destroyed their lodges, and threatened them. A young man, Two Crows, wanted to bond with the chief's daughter, Red Rose. The Chief did not approve, saying he wanted a strong, and brave man for his daughter. The chief did not think that Two Crows was strong and brave. The men had gone off hunting, leaving Two Crows behind. Red Rose came running from the river with a large black bear pursuing her. Two Crows grabbed a large spear, placing himself in front of the charging bear. The charging bear impaled himself upon the spear held by Two Crows.

When the hunting party returned, the chief, seeing the dead large bear, asked, "Who killed this bear?"

Red Rose responded, "The brave and strong man who I will bond with, Two Crows."

The chief, hearing the many women verifying the feat, pronounced Two Crows a brave and strong man. Two Crows and Red Rose shared the hide of the bear for many years, having many children. In time, Two Crows became the chief. So became the tradition of a boy killing a bear, establishing his place as a man. Snow wondered, could he be brave?

As he neared the crazy woman's lodge, she stepped out, accosting Snow. She gave him something wrapped in a bit of hide, saying, "Hide this under your tunic. It is powerful medicine for a man true of heart. I know that you are true at heart. Go now. Show it to no one. Leave me be." This was disturbing to Snow; The crazy woman did not talk to anyone. He put the package under his tunic, going to his lodge.

Snow's mother was in the lodge, packing food and medicine for his journey. It must have been the expression on his face. His mother asked, "What is wrong, Snow?"

"I do not know. The crazy woman gave me a package. She talked to me. She said to not tell or show anyone."

"What did she give you?"

Snow pulled the package from under his tunic, laid it down on the ground, and carefully unwrapped it. It was a knife, the likes that was unknown to Snow or his mother. Snow picked it up. It fit comfortably in his hand. He pulled the blade out of its sheath. It was smooth, with wavy lines that were alternately dark and light gray in color. It was the length of half his forearm. The hilt was made of what looked like an enormous tooth with strange symbols carved on it.

Snow touched its edge. When he withdrew his finger, a drop of blood dripped from a clean cut.

Snow tried to hand it to his mother, hilt first. His mother refused to touch the knife, saying, "Let me get the shaman to look at this knife." While his mom was gone, Snow hefted the knife. It seemed to fit his hand. It felt good. It was a wonderful weapon.

His mother returned with the shaman. The shaman asked Snow to lay the knife on a hide on the ground. Snow told the story of the crazy woman and the knife. The shaman examined the knife without touching it. He slowly ran his hands over it.

The shaman finely said, "This is powerful medicine from a land far away. Keep it hidden. Let an enemy only see it as it cuts them. Speak of this to no one."

Snow asked, "Is it cursed?"

"Only to the person that bleeds from its cut."

Mother ordered, "Snow, put it away. Do as the shaman asks. I have never seen it."

Snow was off, heading toward the mountains, north, toward the Big Dipper, he would look for bear sign that would decide his direction. He was not far from the village when he heard a familiar call. It was Little Rose.

"Come out, Little Rose. Please do not shame me."

The skinny girl came out from behind a bush. She handed Snow a small decorated bag, saying, "I want you to take this with you. With it, I will be with you." She disappeared into the brush.

It was her personal medicine bag. All people had one. It contained what a person cherished that gave them strength. What a person had in their bag was no one's business. Snow had his bag. It contained a tooth from the first deer he killed, a special stone he had found that sparkled red, the front two teeth from a badger that he killed, and a few beads that were his grandmother's. Snow had a problem. He could not go back to return the medicine bag. He could not return to the village until he had completed his quest. It was valuable to Little Rose, so he could not throw it away; that would bring bad luck. The skinny girl was like a sharp small stone in his moccasin. Good riddance to her for a while. If she tried to follow, she would be bear bait.

Snow had walked all day uphill, he was near the tree line, he had not seen any bear sign. He did manage to get a rabbit for dinner. He found a spot between two large rocks where he could safely sleep. He would point his spears toward the opening in case he had any unwanted guests during the night. As Snow enjoyed his small fire, cooked his rabbit, he thought, here on the hillside were blueberries, cranberries, and crowberries. Bears like berries. Tomorrow, he should find bear sign.

The next morning, Snow started walking along the tree line east toward the rising sun, there was an abundance of berries. When Snow saw an especially nice patch of blueberries or cranberries, he would stop, fill his mouth, then pick a handful to eat as he walked. He also chewed on some of the dried meat his mother had packed for him. He had walked all day, seeing no bear sign. He had managed to shoot a spruce hen for supper. He had drunk all his water. There were no ponds or streams for water this high up the mountainside. Up a little higher, he saw a ravine that looked to have some snow in it. Snow went up, ate some snow, and gathered enough to fill his water bag.

Being above the tree line, he looked about. He had never been this high before. The view was spectacular. He could see how big his world was. Looking down into the valley, he could see sections of the river where it twisted through the valley. He had a good view of the mountains on the other side of the valley. Looking in the direction of the rising sun, he could see the High Lake. He had heard of it but never went that far, nor had he seen it before. It was a long way off. Some of his cousins had a village at the High Lake. It was called the Lake Village. Looking toward the setting sun, he could see where the river went out into the prairie. The far edge of the prairie could not be seen. It just looked to blend into the horizon. Snow had been told that there was another village of his kin near a lake not far from the prairie. It was called Red Rock Village, named for a cliff of red rock near it. He could not see that lake. Looking toward the Big Dipper, Snow could see that he was not yet near the top of the mountain.

Snow looked carefully, hoping to spot a bear on the hillside. No bear sign. Back to the tree line to make camp for the night, where he would cook his spruce hen.

Toward afternoon on the next day, Snow came across what looked like a game trail diagonally heading uphill. He was getting low on water. There might be snow along this trail. Walking up the trail, he looked at the view. It looked the same as yesterday. It was like he had not traveled far. Snow noticed that he got short of breath as he climbed. Snow spotted some animals ahead. At first it was a mystery what he was seeing. As he got closer, he realized they were sheep. He had seen drawings of them and had heard some of the older men talking of them. Some of them had magnificent curved horns. Snow tried to put a sneak on them. They would not let him get within bow range. It was getting late. He saw snow in a crevice below him, but still no bear sign. He managed to shoot a jackrabbit. It would be tough eating it though. Better than nothing. There seemed to be an abundance of berries even up here, though the berries seemed smaller and spaced farther apart up here. It looked like Snow was still not near the top of the mountain.

The next day, Snow continued to walk along the tree line. By midafternoon, he came across a site where there were fragments of bones strewed about. Then he saw a spearhead with a rotten shaft. Looking about, there was a rotting bow, the remains of an arrow quiver, shredded leather pants, tunic, and other artifacts. This was the site where a man had met his end. The way the clothing was ripped and shredded, as well as how the larger bones had been cracked open, Snow concluded a bear was responsible. Snow gathered up what bone fragments he found and other artifacts, stacked them up, then piled rocks on top. He placed the spearhead and arrowheads that he found on the pile of rocks. Snow said a chant, asking the great spirits to accept this hunter into their world.

Snow shot another spruce hen and found a little snow behind some rocks that made some shade. As he cooked his dinner, Snow thought that the remains he found could be his brother.

Snow decided that if he went lower, more into the thicker forest, he might find bear sign. After another three days of walking,

Snow found a rotten log that had been ripped apart. It was where a bear had looked for grubs in the rotten wood. Snow guessed that it was no more than a few days old by how little the wood that had been ripped apart and shredded had dried. The size of the claw marks indicated it was a bear near the size of his father's bear. This was what he was looking for, a good bear. The tracks went uphill. It was late. Tomorrow, Snow would try to follow the sign in good light.

For the first few days of Snow's journey his spirits had soared, seeing all the new sights and feeling his independence. The last couple of days seemed to be repeats of the previous days. Again, Snow's spirits soared in anticipation. He had found good bear sign.

It was hard following the tracks in the rocky ground. By looking carefully at a slight distance, Snow could see where the bear had nipped at the berries or an occasional claw mark in spots of soft ground. It appeared the bear was like him, enjoying a mouthful of berries to chew on. It was hard to see the sign; the going was slow. Snow found some droppings. They were not fresh. The bear was mainly eating barriers. After one day's hike, Snow was well above the tree line but not to the top.

By midmorning the next day, Snow came across a winter-killed sheep. The bear also had found it, filling his stomach on rotten meat. The bear had spent some time here cracking bones for the rich marrow that they contained. By late afternoon, it was easy tracking the bear. He had climbed to where the snow was spotty. In the snow, it looked as if the tracks were several days old by the amount of snow melting around the tracks. Snow wondered how far up was the top of this mountain. Normal walking started to labor his breathing. Snow had come this far; he was not yet ready to turn back. The grass, lichen, and small shrubs here did not support a fire for long. The areas that had no snow were covered with a colorful array of flowers. Sleeping was difficult. It was cold, and there was no cover.

By midday the next day, Snow had followed the tracks wadding through knee-deep snow. He reached the summit in a gap between high peaks. Looking out, he could see a vast tract of land. He was above the few clouds that were over the prairie. Below and ahead were smaller mountains. The bear tracks could be seen going down toward a large hill below. It looked like there was heavy woods in the hills below. Snow was at the end of this trail. He was not ready to leave his valley and people. If he continued his pursuit, he might never find his way home. Looking out, Snow realized that his valley was only a small piece of the world. He found a rock to sit upon so he could rest to behold the wonders he was seeing. Out on the prairie, he saw what he thought was a great river snaking its way across the prairie. Was this the great river of legend where his people had come from? The homeland that his ancestors had been driven from by the Redface? He was between two huge mountains, one on either side of him. He was in a pass between them. His valley looked small from up here. He could see several rows of mountains beyond what was the mountains of his valley's south edge. Were there more valleys between the mountains? Snow felt tiny and insignificant. Snow headed back down the way he had come. Snow was not totally disappointed. What he had seen was worth the climb.

It was easier going down than it was coming up. At midafternoon, Snow spotted what he thought to be a bear coming up the mountain. It was toward the rising sun. Snow was above the bear. Snow started to traverse the mountain, hoping to get in front of the bear coming up. At that time, Snow had the high ground. It got dark with no moon before Snow was in position. Again, a night with no fire, dried meat, and fish to eat, along with some berries. Snow had always liked berries, though now he was getting tired of berries.

As soon as the light permitted, Snow was on the move. He was moving in a stalking mode, knowing that there was a bear out there, his quarry. He knew he could easily become breakfast for the bear. Snow had moved to where he thought the bear would be coming up. Had he missed the bear? Had the bear kept moving all night? After a while, he spotted the bear. The bear was down near the tree line, moving away from the area. Why had the bear changed his mind? Where was he going? The bear was moving like he was spooked. Snow saw some movement to his left below him. It was a huge brown bear; the bear was tasting the air with its tongue. The slight breeze was from Snow's right. Snow realized he might be in trouble. Snow was sitting still, hoping the bear did not scent him. The bear was moving from left to right. It would pass right below him. Snow's father's words echoed in his mind, "Do not go high where the giant brown bear lives." Why had he ignored his father's advice? As the huge brute was just below Snow, the bear stopped, stood up on his hind legs, tasted the air, then looked right at Snow with his small, dark beady eyes. Snow realized he would never go home again. Snow resolved that he would do his best to let this bear feel his spearhead in his flesh. Maybe the great spirits would accept him if he stood brave.

The bear was moving slowly toward Snow, testing the air as he came; Snow prepared. His best spear was laid, pointing toward the bear. Looking behind, there was a good anchor rock. Snow placed the butt of the spear shaft against the rock. Snow looked into the bear's dark little eyes. He could hear the bear breathing in a rumbling sound. Snow's father's words echoed in his mind, "Raise your spear at the right time, letting him impale himself." The huge bear was moving slowly toward Snow.

Snow was consumed by a great fear that fed his scream, "Charge me, kill me quickly." The bear charged, Snow raised his spear.

Snow's eyes burned. He tasted blood. His mouth was full of blood. He could hardly breathe. He could not move. Everything hurt. He could not see. So this is death. Snow felt warm all over. There was a sharp pain in his side. Trying to move it felt like he could move his right forearm and hand. Where was he? What had happened? Why was death so painful? Slowly, Snow realized he was under the bear, and the bear was not moving. Snow concluded that he was not dead. He was worse than dead. He was broken and pinned under a huge bear. Slowly, Snow worked himself loose. He had to pull and push and wiggle. Everything hurt. Every move was painful. After a struggle, Snow was free, though in great pain.

Snow found some snow nearby. He used the snow to clear the blood from his eyes. The snow also helped clear the taste of blood from Snow's mouth. Snow felt no exhilaration in this kill. He was on the side of a mountain, alone, and far from home. His food, bow and arrows, and other supplies were under this huge bear. Snow knew that he was injured. He hurt so bad all over. He had so much blood on him, he knew not how bad or how much of the blood was his. Snow leaned against a rock, trying to collect his thoughts. He looked up. The eagles and vultures were already circling above. It was still early in the day. What should he do? What could he do? Should he just wait for the eagles and vultures to pick his bones clean? Snow fell. The knife that the crazy woman gave him was gone, probably under the bear like everything else he owned. After a while, Snow started to clean himself up using the snow.

He mused, "Snow cleaning Snow."

Snow remembered his grandmother saying, "Things were not bad as long as one can find humor."

Snow started to remove rocks and dirt from the side of the bear, making a shallow hole. This let Snow roll the bear over enough so he could get his gear, exposing the bear's belly to start skinning him. Snow's bow was broken from the bear's impact. Arrows were of no good without a bow. Snow finally found the crazy woman's knife. It was not broken. Snow started skinning the bear. He could not roll the bear around, having to cut his way through. Soon Snow was surrounded by scavengers of every type as Snow threw pieces of bear aside. The sun was setting; he could do no more. He moved away from the bear, collapsing in exhaustion.

As daylight came, Snow was awakened by the squawks of hundreds of birds fighting over the right to take their share of the bear's carcass. Snow found it hard to move; he hurt all over. Four wolves wanted his bear. Snow used his remaining spear to prod the wolves away. Snow went to work, throwing pieces of the bear at the wolves. The wolves just wanted a meal. By midmorning he cut and removed the bear's heart from around his spear's shank. Snow's spearhead had pierced through the center of the bear's heart and continued into his entrails. Snow cut off a piece of heart, having lunch. The rest of the heart, he wrapped in a piece of deer hide for later. Snow had to cut the bear into pieces to remove it from its hide. By dusk Snow had the hide separated from the bear. The crazy woman's knife made the job easier. The hide was too heavy for Snow to carry more than a few feet if he was at his best, which he was not. Snow dragged the hide aside, wrapping himself in it to keep warm and slept. The next day

Snow struggled down to the tree line where he cut poles for a skid. By evening he had cut two poles for a skid, built a fire warming himself, and cooked some of the bear's heart. He ate and again slept. The next day Snow struggled to return to the kill site dragging the poles he had cut. Snow spent another night wrapped in his bear hide. It took the entire next day to drag the hide down to the tree line using the two poles as a drag. Here he had enough wood for a campfire. The fire would keep the wolves away. Snow cooked the last of the bear's heart, eating it in the hope that the spirit of the bear would become part of him, as was the custom.

The next day, Snow made little progress. He rested up, tending his wounds. He was back in the thin woods near the tree line where he felt at home; the day was pleasant. Snow had lost track of how long he had been gone. He tried to remember what his village looked like; he could not exactly remember. He tried to envision White Dove; he could not clearly see her in his mind. Snow tried to see himself presenting his bear hide to White Dove, proposing bonding as one. She was beautiful and strong. She would make a good wife. He had been gone a long time; maybe Red Hawk or Big Badger had already returned and won her with a bear hide. That night Snow dreamed of Little Rose. When Snow awoke, he took Little Rose's medicine bag, holding it in his hand. Had she cast a spell over him? How could he break the spell? Was it her medicine bag? She was skinny and had little tits. Snow could not bring himself to throw her bag away. Snow wondered, had Little Rose's medicine helped guide his spear deep into the bear?

Snow set off for home, dragging his trophy behind him. How many days from home? How many days had he been gone? It was confusing; he was not sure. He needed water. Should he go up for snow or go down into the thick woods where the travel would be harder? He set his load aside, going up for snow. It was getting warmer; the snow was higher and scarcer. Maybe it would rain so small rivulets would form where water could be collected.

The next day it started to rain. It rained hard. There was thunder and lightning. Then it hailed. Snow got wet and cold; it rained so hard that without a shelter, a fire could not be made. Snow wrapped himself into his bear hide and slept. It rained hard for two days.

Snow tried to keep moving. Snow was looking for a line of large rocks that marked the trail to his village. It turned foggy. Snow could not see far enough to see the rocks. He did not want to pass up the trail. Using the bear hide as a cover, he made a small shelter where he managed to get a fire going. It gave Snow a sense of well-being. Snow felt that home was a faraway dream. The fire warmed him; home was where he was.

In a few days, Snow found the rocks that marked his path home. He again tried to envision White Dove with her smile, her rounded hips, and her prominent breasts. He just could not get it right. The image was blurred in his mind. Snow stopped to camp. He was a half day away from home. It did not take long to snare a rabbit and build a fire. Snow wanted to prepare himself for home. He was not the same person who had left. Snow did not know who he was anymore. The bear hide he brought would define him as a great hunter; he did not feel like a great hunter. He just wanted to sit on the river bank, watch the water go by, and maybe spear a couple of fish.

By midday, Snow pulled his load into the village. Before he reached the center of the village, he was surround by villagers asking him many confusing questions. He dropped the poles supporting the load in front of his father's lodge. Snow was home.

Snow's mother, Spring Flower, wrapped her arms around her son. She began to weep in joy.

The chief soon showed up, asking, "What do you bring?"

Snow responded, not in the voice of a successful hunter returning, but in the voice of a man who was used up. He knew the right words to say. "I bring the hide of a bear that I killed, and I ate its heart. I take my place as a member of the council."

The chief said, "Show us this hide of a bear."

Snow proceeded to untie the hide, unfolding it. He was helped by his mother and sisters. Many had to step back to make room for the hide to be fully displayed. There were many voices of amazement. Snow did not hear them.

The chief announced, "Welcome to the council of the River Village. To all, this is Snow, a member of our council. Does anyone dispute Snow's place on the council?" There were no protests.

CHAPTER 2

People touched and admired Snow's bear hide. It was not long till Red Hawk and Big Badger showed up. They took a look at the bear hide on the ground. They looked at Snow; then they turned, walking away.

Snow asked, "Mom, why did they walk away. What is wrong?"

Mother answered, "Nothing is wrong. They both got nice bears." *Nice bear* meant that they were small and nothing special.

Snow asked, "Have they bonded with a woman?" Snow noticed White Dove. She was smiling, with a demeanor that said, "Am I not pretty?" She was not as pretty as Snow remembered.

Mother said, "You have been gone a long time. Much has changed, Yes, Red Hawk has bonded with Red Blossom. Big Badger has bonded with Sweet Clove. White Dove is still available, if that is what you are asking. I am sure that she would be happy to lie with you on your big, brown bear hide."

Snow looked at White Dove. She was knelt down, caressing the brown fur. Snow wondered what White Dove wanted. Snow noticed Little Rose among the crowd. He thought of her medicine bag that he still carried. What did she want?

Snow was tired, clear down into his innards. His tunic, trousers, and moccasins were bloodstained and worn beyond repair. Snow stood slouched over, then collapsed to his knees. Except for the big brown bear hide, he looked a frightful sight, not even a bow and quiver.

Mom said, "Snow, come with me. We will get you cleaned up and some good food in your stomach. The women will tend to your bear hide. You are home." Mom wrapped her arm around Snow, helped him up, and took him into their lodge.

As his mom held him tight, Snow grimaced. "Not so hard, Mom, my ribs hurt." Mom fed, cleaned up, and pampered Snow.

They had a special council to honor Snow, wanting to hear his story. Snow did not show. The council members protested. The wives and mothers said to let the man sleep. The council postponed their meeting. Snow slept through to morning.

A good night's sleep, good food, security, and comfort of the village made Snow feel that he was home. Snow was now a man, and as such, he could take a wife. The tradition was that he would take his bear hide and offer it to the girl of his choice. If she accepted the hide, she would be his betrothed. A ceremony would be held in five days; the village would try to keep them apart until the ceremony of joining. The five days gave the bride time to build a lodge and prepare the bear hide for them to lie on together. The other women in the village would help the bride, but it was her responsibility to provide the lodge and keep their bed.

Snow's mother asked, "Snow, how long do you plan to make the village wait for you to present your bear hide?"

Snow answered, "I have never promised White Dove. I have not made a choice for a wife. How do I decide?"

Mother said, "When you took off your tunic, I noticed you had two medicine bags. Is the second bag White Dove's?"

"The bag is Little Rose's medicine bag. As I left on my hunt, she followed me into the woods where she gave me her medicine bag. Then she fled before I could return it to her."

Mother asked, "Snow, who would you trust with your medicine bag?"

With help, Snow struggled with his bear hide over his shoulders; even when it had partly dried out and was fleshed, it was all he could handle. With determination, he walked along the circular row of lodges, struggling under the weight of the hide. He was followed by villagers wanting to witness the event.

White Dove, with her family, was in front of her father's lodge, looking confident and smug. After Snow passed her, she screamed,

"What is wrong with you? Where are you going?" This was the third time she had been recently jilted.

Snow stopped in front of Little Rose's father's lodge. Little Rose was standing next to her father. Snow looked upon Little Rose. She looked into Snow's eyes. What she saw in his eyes made her weak in the legs. Her heart pounded in her chest. Her wildest dream came true when Snow said, "Little Rose, will you accept this bear hide so we can lie together on it in our own lodge?"

Little Rose stepped forward, saying, "I will accept this bear hide. I will lie on it with you, keep your lodge, and bear you children." In excitement, Little Rose grabbed ahold of the hide and pulled to put it on her shoulders. Little Rose and Snow went to the ground under the hide's weight. Her father, mother, two younger brothers, along with some of the crowd that was following Snow came to their rescue, lifting the hide off them. All laughed but Little Rose. Her big moment with most of the village watching became a humorous story to be retold for years at many bonfires.

Snow went with his father to council. His father told him of the proper etiquette of the council meetings. He sat near the entrance farthest from the chief and shaman. This was his proper place in the council, being the most junior member. He sat next to Red Hawk and Big Badger. Snow's father, who sat next to the chief, stood, motioning for Snow to stand.

"I present Snow as a member of this council. Does anyone challenge Snow?" No one said a word. Snow was now accepted in council.

The chief stood. "Snow, would you tell us of your bear hunt?"

Snow said, "I went north to the tree line and walked toward the rising sun for days. I could find no bear sign. I saw other game, including the bighorn sheep. I finally found bear sign, it was a good-sized bear. The tracks went uphill, so I followed for a couple of days. The tracks led me into waist-deep snow. The bear tracks went down the other side of the mountain toward the prairie."

Snow was interrupted, he was asked if he has seen the prairie. Then he was asked to describe what he had seen. As he told his story, many times he was asked to tell more. Snow did not consider himself a good storyteller. He was uncomfortable. He was finally at the place in the story where he was confronted by his bear.

"I was trying to get in front of the large black bear when he turned, running off down the hill. I realized the large black bear was being hunted by a huge brown bear that I had not seen that had been waiting near me. I tried to hide. The brown bear scented me. I knew I was going to be his dinner. I wanted for him to feel the tip of my spear before I felt his teeth and claws in my flesh. He charged, I raised my spear, than my world went dark. I awoke under the bear, thinking I was dead, covered in his blood and pinned to the ground. He had killed himself on my spear." Snow sat down to a quiet council, thinking himself as lucky that he did not die; not the great hunter, but the lucky hunter.

The chief stood. "It takes the bravest of men standing their ground, facing their death." As the chief sat, there was many affirmative "Uhs," an expression of approval.

The meeting was adjourned. Snow was overwhelmed with welcomes to the council.

Later, Snow's father told him, "Most men pound their chests pronouncing themselves as brave hunters. Your modesty and honesty made all reflect on themselves. The chief's words made all reflect on what is bravery. I am proud of you."

Little Rose, with the help of many women of the village, cleaned, fleshed, and tanned the hide by rubbing it with the sap from tamarack trees, then a thorough rinsing, then drying. Little Rose walked with the chief to select a site for their lodge. She selected a site at the edge of the village near the crazy old woman's small hut. The chief approved.

The chief asked, "Why do you want your lodge near the crazy old woman's hut?"

Little Rose said, "She needs a neighbor looking out for her, and I know she will look out for us. She is part of our village."

Snow was accepting the five-day wait. It gave him time to heal, fish, and think. He was wondering why he had made the choice he had made. Had she put a spell on him with her medicine bag? She was skinny and had small breasts. He had never had nooky. She had little breasts and was skinny. How would she be with nooky? Would she like nooky? At least he would have a good hunting partner. She did not talk a lot of nonsense like some of the other girls.

Snow's dad went fishing with him. Snow got some fatherly advice. "Always listen to your wife. You do not have to do what she says, but listen to her. If she wants to yell at you, listen to her. If you want nooky, pretend that you just want to hold her. Never disagree or correct her in public. That is also good advice in private too. If you can treat her like she is special to you, you will be special to her, and she will be special to you. No matter how bad her cooking or cleaning or anything else, remember that it is always wonderful, like her. My father gave me the same advice I am giving you. I have a good marriage, most of the time, to your mostly wonderful mother. My last advice, on your first night together, be gentle. Go slowly. She will know what to do better than you."

Snow asked, "What can I do safely?"

"Go hunting and fishing."

"Little Rose goes hunting with me."

"Then go fishing."

Little Rose worked hard for five days. Not only was she responsible for the largest bear hide anyone had ever seen, she had to build a lodge that was big enough for a huge bear hide. She also had to get ready for her joining ceremony. In a few hours, she would be joined with Snow. The roof of the lodge needed more work. It would probably leak when it rained. The bear hide was not completely dry.

Little Rose sat in the middle of the lodge getting a wet rear end from the damp bear hide. She realized that in a matter of hours, she would be expected to make her husband happy, giving him nooky. She wanted nooky, too, but it scared her. She wondered if it would work. Her mother had told her what to expect. She had heard the older women talking of how much it hurt the first time and how some men were rough and demanding. Little Rose was to go to her father's lodge to get ready for the ceremony. She was to go and bathe. Her hair was to be washed, brushed, and braided. She had to put on her finest clothes. Instead of getting ready, she was sitting in the lodge she had built for her husband with tears running down her cheeks.

This was supposed to be the happiest day of her life. She would have a respected and strong husband, one that all the unbonded girls wanted. Little Rose felt like a scared little girl.

Her mother came to talk to her. "Little Rose, I was afraid when I was bonded. I think that Snow is probably scared too. I also think that Snow is a good man who will be a good husband for you. Tonight, talk to him. Tell him how you feel. Ask him to please be gentle and take time so both of you can enjoy each other. I think that Snow is a man who will listen to you."

Snow's mother told him to wait until all had time to get to the bonfire before he made his entrance. As he grew up, he had witnessed many joining ceremonies. He was nervous. He went over in his head many times the words he was to say. As he walked to the bonfire, he felt his legs quiver, and his stomach growled at him. He was supposed to feel good. Tonight, he would have a wife and get nooky. He actually was full of apprehension.

Snow walked, trying to look strong and brave. He stood next to the bonfire with his spear pointed up to the sky. All eyes were on Snow.

"I, Snow, son of Soaring Raven and Spring Flower, say that I am a member of council. I have presented to Little Rose my bear hide, which she accepted. I claim her as my wife. Does anyone challenge my claim?" There were no challengers.

Little Rose stepped next to the bonfire. All eyes were on her, including Snow's. She raised her hand with a stone knife in it, saying, "I, Little Rose, daughter of Great Eagle and Blue Bird, have accepted Snow's bear hide. I built him a lodge and made a bed of his bear hide for us to lie on. I claim Snow as my husband. Does anyone challenge my claim?" No one challenged.

Snow and Little Rose stepped forward facing each other. Little Rose took her knife, cutting the palm of her left hand. Show held out his right hand, Little Rose cut his palm. They held their bleeding palms up for all to see. Then Snow and Little Rose held their bleeding palms together, interlaced their fingers.

Snow spoke, "As our blood flows together, we are one."

Little Rose spoke, "As our blood flows together, we are one."

The shaman stood and tied their joined hands with a leather thong, saying, "Snow and Little Rose have joined and are now greater than the sum of both of them separate."

The villagers made two lines, which Snow and Little Rose walked between, bloody hand in bloody hand, toward their lodge.

Upon entering their lodge, still hand in hand, bound together dripping blood; Snow headed his father's words, he placed his free arm around Little Rose saying, "You have built us a solid lodge and made us a great bead."

"The roof needs work, and the bed is still wet."

"You cut really deep."

"The deeper the cut, the deeper the bond. Let me wrap your hand."

"That can be later. Now, I just want to hold you."

Little Rose wrapped their joined hands in some woven cloth to stop the blood dripping. They lay down together on their damp bed, arms wrapped around each other. Snow told Little Rose how wonderful she was. Little Rose told Snow how brave and strong he was. With their free hands they touched each other, feeling each other. They were awakening strong emotions in each other. Their lips touched; then their lips touched each other's skin. They each got braver and started to touch each other in ways that were new to them. They explored each other's body. Eventually, Little Rose unbound their hands so that they could remove each other's clothing. Snow wanted to just take Little Rose, but he resisted his urges. He enjoyed touching and being touched. Little Rose lay on her back, spread her legs, then pulled Snow on top of her, saying, "I want you to take me."

Snow woke up on a damp bear hide with a fur blanket over him. He heard the sound of a woman humming a melody. Looking up, he could see beams of light pouring through holes in the roof over him. His hand was wrapped and was tender to the touch. He smiled deep down. His clothes were neatly folded next to him. He got dressed to find his wife on top of the lodge, patching holes in the roof.

Seeing Snow, Little Rose climbed down, saying, "I will get you breakfast, my brave husband." She already had breakfast ready. The bread was hard, chewy, and lacked flavor; the roast rabbit was dried out and tough.

Snow complimented, "The breakfast is good."

Little Rose apologized, "I am sorry. The bread is hard and tastes bad, and I overcooked the rabbit, ruining it."

Snow said, "Let me help you fix the roof. Then we can go hunting." So was the start of their life together. Snow started to realize how wise his father's words were and how wonderful Little Rose was.

Snow explained to Little Rose the strange knife that he carried under his tunic. They talked and made promises to each other. They were simple rules that Little Rose's mother told her she had made with her husband. They would always be honest with each other and would be loyal. Little Rose agreed that it was acceptable if Snow told her small fibs about her cooking, and Little Rose was allowed to fib a little to Snow to not hurt his feelings. Snow did not need to hear how much he farted in his sleep and how bad they smelled.

Their bed dried out, the roof was sealed up, and their hands healed. Snow made two bows, one for each of them. Little Rose became an accomplished archer. Not all the people of the village approved of Little Rose using a bow and Snow teaching her to use a bow. Nobody complained when they brought in fresh game and gave it to others. Little Rose did little cooking. Why cook when you have fresh game to trade for prepared meals? Snow was known to do a lot of women's work—helping build lodges, skinning animals, and cleaning hides. They started to set an example not by their words but by their deeds. Some of the girls asked their fathers to help them make bows then teach them how to use them. Most fathers had a hard time saying no to their daughters when they asked nicely and smiled, looking into their eyes. Mothers were making their sons help in lodge building. It was slow, but people's opinions were changing. The shaman again warned that hard times were coming. He approved of women and girls learning to use weapons. There were old stories that were retold of the women of the tribe fighting alongside their men when they were at war with the Redface.

To not deplete the game near their village, Little Rose and Snow started to travel farther from the village. Sometimes they would be gone for several days. They enjoyed the adventure. They went up to the tree line. Little Rose wanted to go to the top of the mountain. Snow did not want to take her there, warning her of the big brown bears. Little Rose was persuasive. Snow found it hard saying no to his wife. She did make him happy. Snow agreed that their next trip would be to the top of the mountain. Snow insisted that they both carry large spears and go well equipped.

After three days of walking, they found some snow in shady areas even though it was midsummer. They both found that they became short of breath the higher they climbed. The views were spectacular. They often stopped to catch their breath and enjoy the views. Snow became a little bit of a pest, continually warning to watch for bears. They spotted a herd of bighorn sheep. Without cover, they could not get close enough for a shot. The sheep seemed to balance on a narrow ledge of rock or scurry up a steep grade strewn with rocks with ease.

Little Rose commented, "What magnificent animals. It was worth the climb to just see them."

When nearing the top of the pass, the snow was getting deeper; some places they were walking on hard ice. The grade was steep; it took a lot of physical exertion. They found some cover in a crevasse and spent the night. It was cold, so they cuddled up close to share body heat. They lay looking up at the stars. They both agreed that they had never seen so many stars before. The stars were so thick in one streak that they looked like a cloud. The next day, the climb was hard. It was steep; they had to work their way around icy spots to find good footing. The very top was rounded; the walking got easier. They stopped and marveled as they looked out over the prairie.

Snow said, "I know that this pass is higher than the pass I reached a few months before."

They could plainly see the great river snaking itself through the prairie. They looked down on the top of a few sparsely spread clouds.

Little Rose said, "According to legend, the prairie and river was our ancestral home. Our ancestors were driven out of their homes, retreating to our valley."

Snow commented, "We are in a pass. Look how high the mountains are on either side of us."

Little Rose speculated, "I wonder if we could touch the stars from on top of those mountains?"

It was getting late, so they decided to spend the night. There was no wood to build a fire, so they would have a cold camp. They moved a few rocks around to make a flat spot to sleep. They snuggled into their fur blankets and snuggled closer and closer. They enjoyed each other as husband and wife; they truly felt a oneness.

When it got really dark out, Little Rose looked out over the prairie, asking, "Are those bonfires on the prairie?"

They got up, observing what they believed to be fires. By their location, they believed they were along the great river. They counted nine fires spaced across the prairie. Looking on the other side of the mountain, toward the setting sun direction, they saw one more fire.

Snow said, "That might be close to where our valley's river enters into the prairie, not far from the Red Rock Village. We will have to look in the morning."

In the morning, looking, they agreed that the fire they saw was not far from the Red Rock Village. They also looked out over the prairie. Little Rose spotted a small trail of smoke coming up from a spot down below them in the hills between the prairie and mountains. They talked and decided that they needed to tell the village elders.

They were not far down the mountain when at the same time they spotted a large brown bear down below. Little Rose wanted to continue and go around. Snow was adamant that they stay and watch the bear from a concealed position. They moved as one; they were able to communicate with gestures and signs. They used an outcropping of rocks to conceal their presence. While they were waiting, they had a herd of bighorn sheep walk just below them. Little Rose wanted to take one. Snow signaled no. He did not want to attract the bear. By midday the bear had moved off toward the direction of the setting sun. Little Rose and Snow headed down making the tree line by nightfall. They keep a close watch for the brown bear. Going down was a lot easier than climbing up.

In the morning, Little Rose got a shot on a young buck. They would not go back empty-handed. It always amazed Snow how strong his skinny wife was. They put the deer on a pole. Little Rose carried her share of the burden. By evening they made it back to the village.

Snow told the chief what they had seen. The chief called a council meeting. At the council, Snow told what he and Little Rose had seen.

The shaman warned, "This is not good. I fear that our people's old enemy is coming. We should prepare."

The Chief asked, "Snow, can you go and warn the people of the Red Rock Village? Tell them your story. Who will go with Snow?"

Soaring Raven, Snow's father, answered, "I will go with Snow to the village of the Red Rock." After the meeting, Snow's father asked, "Why did you go to the top of the mountains?"

Snow answered, "Little Rose wanted to see the prairie. I followed your advice, listening to my wife."

"It is good to listen, but you do not always need to obey."

In the morning, on the trail to the village of the Red Rock, Soaring Raven said, "I am surprised that Little Rose is coming with us."

Snow replied, "I followed your advice. I listened to my wife. She said she was coming with us. I did not say anything. I just listened." It was a long day's walk on the good path.

Toward late afternoon, Little Rose asked, "Should we bring some fresh game with us?"

Soaring Raven said, "It would be a good gesture to not arrive empty-handed."

Little Rose disappeared into the woods. It was not long until there was a birdcall coming from their right. Snow motioned to his father to be still, readying an arrow in his bow. Shortly, two does and one fawn stepped out of the woods in front of them. Snow shot at the doe that did not have the fawn following. Snow's shot was true, the doe bolted, ran a way down the trail in front of them, soon falling over. Little Rose rejoined them.

Soaring Raven commented, "Now I know why you do not hunt with me anymore."

As they entered the village, Soaring Raven was recognized. Soon they were greeted by the Red Rock chief. Soaring Raven introduced his son, Snow, and Snow's wife, Little Rose.

The chief asked, "Snow, are you the one who killed a big brown bear?"

Snow replied, "The bear killed himself on my spear."

The chief asked, "Were you holding the spear?"

Snow replied, "I do not remember, it happened fast, I was knocked unconscious."

The chief replied, "Yes, I understand."

Soaring Raven said, "We have been sent here by our chief and shaman because they have concerns that an old enemy might be approaching."

The chief asked, "Is this for our council?"

Soaring Raven replied, "Yes, we would like to address your council."

Little Rose went with the women who took their deer. She got a lot of attention from the girls and younger women. They had never seen a woman carrying a bow and arrows. A girl of about ten years old asked if she was accurate. Little Rose pointed to a pine cone in a tree, drew her bow, and brought the pine cone down. The girl retrieved the pine cone with her arrow in it. Some of the men scoffed at a woman with a bow, others accepted it. The girl who asked Little Rose if she was accurate brought her father over, telling him that she wanted a bow, please, hugging her father, looking up into his eyes.

They had the council meeting late afternoon. The chief gave a greeting and introduction.

Soaring Raven said, "I was sent as a representative of the River Village Council. This is Snow. As a member of the River Village Council, he would like to speak to you."

Snow got many "Uhs" grunts, which was a sign of acknowledgment and respect. Snow told of the fires he had seen on the prairie and the one near Red Rock. The council discussed the issue. They decided to continue the discussion the following evening after thought. Then Snow was asked to tell the story of his bear hunt. The chief asked if first a small group could go up to the top of the Red

Cliff to look out onto the prairie for signs of fire in the dark. Two local men would escort Snow and Soaring Raven to the cliff top. Not to the liking of the local men, Little Rose would also go. Snow explained that she had been with him when he saw the fires from the mountaintop. They were not used to women taking an active role in scouting.

They lit torches, going up the path that was narrow and steep, with some places having drop-offs. When they reached the top, the torches were placed behind some rocks. When they looked out, there was what looked like a large campfire with several other smaller cooking fires. It definitely looked like a campsite. The local men explained that there was a lake at the edge of the prairie. The camp looked to be just beyond the lake. The local men pointed out a fire below that was their fish camp on their lake.

They went back down, reporting their findings. Though it was getting late, Snow had several requests that he told the story of his bear hunt at their bonfire. Snow told the story; Little Rose had never heard the whole story, just parts of it, before.

After Snow was done, the consensus was that he was a good storyteller. Little Rose asked, "Snow, why did you tell the story, making it sound like your bear killed himself?"

Snow replied, "Because I was just real lucky. The great spirits are saving me for something. I should have died." They slept in the common lodge.

In the morning, they returned to the Red Cliff top. From there, they could see the lake and river. They also could see some small smoke plumes coming from what was probably a camp. The camp looked to be a day's walk away. They returned to the village to report. They found the entire village preparing for war. They were informed that the small camp on the lakeshore for fishing had been attacked late last night; two had escaped. A war party was sent to investigate.

The chief asked Little Rose if she could teach some of the women to shoot a bow.

Soaring Raven and Snow helped make spears and arrows. The entire village was working on weapons, food, or other tasks.

The Red Rock shaman said, "Our people have lived in peace for ten generations. All we know of war is from stories."

In the afternoon, the war party returned. The camp was destroyed. There was one survivor, a ten-year-old boy who was out tending his rabbit snares in some brambles. From a hiding place in the brambles, he witnessed the raid. The boy said that the attackers had their faces painted red. All their people were dead or taken as slaves. The village became a frenzy of emotions. Some lost loved ones. They were grieving. Some wanted to immediately attack, desiring vengeance; some wanted to prepare for war; and some wanted to retreat up the river to regroup. The chief gathered a small group of respected men, including Soaring Raven, and conducted a war council. A war council had not been declared in generations. After the war council, Soaring Raven said that they had to get back to the River Village. On the way, he explained that, the Red Rock Village was going to get ready for defense, and they had a backup plan for evacuation. They walked until dark and then camped. They finish their trip in the morning.

Returning to their village, Soaring Raven met with the chief and a couple other men. It was declared a war council. Their village would prepare for war. A messenger would be sent to the Lake Village farther up the valley, telling them of the situation. A small group of men would be sent to the Red Rock Village to help them prepare and help them in defense in case of an attack. Snow went by himself to the crazy old woman. She was outside her hut, sewing a buckskin tunic.

Snow asked, "May I sit here with you?" He got a nod of approval. Snow sat. He asked, "I want you to know that the Redface have attacked the Red Rock Village, killing many and taking others as slaves." The crazy woman looked down at her work, shaking her head.

Snow then asked, "I have heard that you know things about the Redface."

Still looking down, she nodded yes.

Snow said, "I am going to fight the Redface. Can you tell me anything that will help me?"

She nodded yes. Snow patiently waited for her advice.

"Burn their privates. Gouge out and burn their eyes. Let the other Redface see what has been done to them. That will give them great fear. They will go to the great spirits as blind women. Women slaves that do not serve them well have their eyes gouged out. A blind woman is the lowest of low. They are to be beaten and abused regularly. Whatever is burnt is lost forever. If you burn their bodies, they are lost forever. Better to send them to the great spirits to suffer an eternity as a blind woman. The Redface are not afraid to die. They are afraid of going to eternity as a blind woman."

Snow responded, "Thank you."

The crazy woman held up her hand. Snow waited. "They like to attack when the moon is bright, with their faced painted red, giving their enemies fear. When they are not killing, they like to build big bonfires, chew crazy leaves, brag about their great deeds until they are drunk and stupid. Then they beat their women. Then they go to bed, sleeping like they are dead. That is the time to attack them. Burn their privates and eyes. Kill all the Redface. Send them to eternity as blind women. Please, now, leave a broken, crazy old woman to her misery."

Snow went and told his father and the chief what the crazy old woman told him. The chief and his father said that they would have no part of gouging out eyes and burning men's privates. Snow agreed.

Eight men, including Snow and his father, Soaring Raven, were sent to the Red Rock Village. The whole village went to work preparing for war. Six young women and older girls banded together. They went to Little Rose, asking her to lead them. They had heard the old stories. They did not want to be slaves of the Redface. They would sooner die fighting.

The Seven Sisters, as they called themselves, started to train together. Other woman helped the men make bows, arrows, and spears. Some weapons, they kept for themselves. The Seven Sisters started to get the attention of the other villagers, including the chief and elders. Other women in the village started to demand their own spears. The men in the village often heard, "I am not going to be a slave." With reluctance and misgivings, the men agreed to train and arm their women. The moon started to get fuller. All had heard that the Redface liked to attack with a bright moon. The crazy old woman started to work with the other women. She seemed to be getting her mind back. She started to tell stories of her life as a young girl and a young woman with the Redface. Even the older women wanted their own spears.

The Red Rock Village council evacuated most of the children and women with small children. The people from the Red Rock Village were accepted into the lodges of the River Village; they were one people.

One woman who was well-rounded with child asked for a spear. When asked why she wanted a spear, she replied, "I choose for myself and my unborn child to live free, not to be slaves."

Early one morning, the Seven Sisters snuck out of the village. They left word with some of the other women that they were going to the Red Rock Village to fight. On their way, they took turns practicing, going through the woods quietly and using animal calls to communicate with each other. They also practiced drawing their bows and lunging with their spears. They talked bravely among each other. Their morale was high.

When they reached the Red Rock Village, Snow and two of the men who had daughters that were part of the Seven Sisters demanded that their women go back. The Seven Sisters were just as demanding. The men found it hard to argue with their women when the women said, "Better be dead than a slave of a Redface. If you do not want me to be a slave, raped, and beaten daily, let me fight alongside you." The women of the Red Rock Village were arming themselves.

A few traders moved from village to village, as well as goods they carried all the gossip as well as the news from village to village. Several days earlier, the traders had come with flint to make arrowheads, spearheads, and knives.

At all times, guards were posted to sound the alarm. Many were doing their training at night and slept during the day. Most believed that the Redface would attack at night. A few scouts had been sent out and had not returned. Early at night, Snow and Little Rose, along with a few others, went up to the top of the Red Cliff. There were still the fires of the large camp on the other side of the lake; also there was a smaller fire near where the fish camp had been. The war council was considering attacking the small camp that was near the fish camp.

Snow was doing guard duty; he was stationed to watch the area of thick woods on the slope next to the Red Cliff. Little Rose was nearby. Sometimes she was still a pest, though Snow learned to love his pest. There was a waxing three-quarter moon that was fairly bright. It would be setting in several hours. Snow heard a cricket that he knew was not a cricket. Little Rose was behind and a little to his left. Something was moving in front, slightly below him. It was moving slow and carefully. It was in the shadows; Snow could not make out what it was. A cricket call then a second cricket call—two intruders. Little Rose must be in a position to see better than he was. Her senses seemed to be better than his. There was the faint sound of leaves being moved with the sound of small branches rubbing across something. Then Snow saw a head then a man's hand motioning. Snow readied his bow, then challenged, "Who goes there?"

The response was two men charging with growls. Snow released his arrow. There was the distinctive thud of an arrow hitting its mark. As Snow reached for his spear, there was another distinctive thud of an arrow hitting its mark, accompanied by a scream of pain. Snow's whistle was in his mouth before he drew his bow. Now he blew hard, sounding the warning. His position was already revealed from the scuffle. There was another whistle from the other side of the village approach. The man who Snow shot lay still; the second man who Snow assumed was shot by Little Rose could be seen in the moonlight. He rolled onto his back; he was trying to pull an arrow from his chest. Just as Snow got ready to impale him with his spear, he heard a gasp then a long exhale of air; he lay still. There was hollering from the center on the main path from the lake. It sounded like someone was running through the brush, going away from the village. A few screams of pain from what sounded like it was from the center of the path from the lake. Then all was quiet again. Snow again nestled into his hidden observation spot. There was a soft and long cricket sound. Snow knew that was the nothing-in-sight-stand-fast signal.

The moon set. It got really dark for a while; then the dawn started to break. When it was light enough to see clearly, Snow's relief came, along with Soaring Raven and another man who was a member of the war council. They wanted to see what had happened, hearing his alarm. Within four body lengths lay two men; their faces were painted red. One with an arrow sticking out of his eye socket; the other with an arrow sticking out from his chest at the position of his heart.

Soaring Raven stated, "Two arrows two deaths, you must shoot fast." Just then, Little Rose stepped out from the thick trees.

Snow replied, "One arrow was mine; the other belonged to Little Rose."

Soaring Raven asked, "If it had not been for Little Rose's arrow, how would you have handled the second warrior?"

Snow answered, "With my spear, if I was lucky."

Soaring Raven asked, "If you would have been alone, how would you have handled three warriors?"

Snow answered, "I would have probably died."

Soaring Raven addressed the other man, "Every one of our guards need a guard watching their back."

Back at the village, it was found out that the previous night's attacks were explorations of the village defenses. The guard on the far side who sounded the other alarm was found dead. He was killed with what looked to be a spear. The attack on the path to the lake was by at least four warriors spread out. There, the village lost two men and killed one Redface. Three Redface were dead and three villagers were killed. Later, they were told that there would be three lines of guards. The second line would watch the back of the front guard; the third would watch the back of the second line. All guards would be in teams of at least four or more, positioned to protect each other's back.

Snow and Little Rose talked. They had both killed a Redface in self-defense; their ancestral enemy, people who killed without remorse, and took women as slaves. They deserved to die. They had each taken a human life. Snow and Little Rose agreed they could rejoice in their kills, at the same time have remorse for killing.

CHAPTER 3

Three days had gone by; the moon would be near full. Snow was again on guard duty on the slope next to the Red Cliff. Because of their previous success, he named his own team. Little Rose had his back; the rest of the Seven Sisters had her back. They had practiced as a team; they wanted to stay a team. The moon was halfway up in the sky; Snow was thinking that he was a lucky man with so many women watching his back. He was actually day-dreaming, not keeping alert. A cricket called from behind him. In the moon shadows, he could see numerous objects moving toward him. They were moving slowly, making little sound. Snow had to make a quick decision, there were many intruders. He could wait till they got closer then challenge them, sounding the alarm. Or sound the alarm, alerting everyone, revealing his position, giving him no element of surprise. Snow decided to not wait, challenge, shoot and sound the alarm. Snow knew that no matter what happened to him, his backup would sound the alarm. At the distance they were at now, if they charged, he could get off two arrows.

Snow readied an arrow, challenged, not wanting to shoot a fellow villager. "Who goes there?"

The intruders arose, charging. At the distance, Snow aimed for the large target, the chest. He was rewarded by a distinctive thud. His second arrow hit its mark. He was being overwhelmed. Snow's spear was stuck in the third Redface's chest. He grabbed his knife. He was facing a man with a spear. There were two thuds in quick order. The man with the spear went down. A Redface with an arrow in his shoulder tried to direct his spear at Snow. Snow dove, pushing the spear aside with his left arm while with his right he plunged his knife into the upper abdomen of his opponent; then he twisted the knife up then pulled it out, making a large gaping wound, cutting deeply into the liver, and making a slice through the diaphragm. As Snow retracted the knife, he pushed away from the enemy. Snow quickly spun around, looking for his next opponent. Snow had been so intent on the opponent in front of him. He was not aware of what was happening around him. There were multiple thuds as arrows struck Redface trying to hastily retreat or to regain their feet. There were multiple whistles blowing. Taking a quick survey, Snow determined that there was not much more to do here right now unless another wave attacked.

Turning around, there in the moonlight were seven women lined up with bows. All had an arrow nocked. One raised and drew their bow, then another thud and a scream of pain.

Continuous shouts and screams were coming from the village.

Snow said, “I am going to the village to see if I can help.”

Little Rose responded, “Let’s go.”

It was a short distance to the clearing where the village was. There was a gentle slope to the village where there was total pandemonium. Many, especially the women, were sleeping in the nearby woods with their spears. The Redface were going from one lodge to the next with stone axes and clubs. There was sporadic fighting with small groups of village men defending their lodges. Seven ladies and Snow ran down the incline to where they were in range, formed a line. They shot arrows at the Redface that were looking for victims in the mainly empty lodges. It was not long until a group of the Redface were charging the line of archers. Another group of Redface were charging the wood line where there were other archers. With those archers were many women with spears that were ready to lunge with their spears at the enemy. The Seven Sisters were almost out of arrows. Many people were lying on the ground, both Redface and villagers. The Redface were throwing their spears with deadly accuracy; two of the Seven Sisters had gone down. Even though many Redface had been killed or wounded, the village people looked to be outnumbered, Snow feared the worst; he had no idea as to what to do except to fight on.

A horn blew, then all the standing Redface started to run in retreat, back to where they had come from. There was a pause; it was like every villager needed to catch their breath. Then there was a wave of activity; the wounded villagers were being helped as the wounded Redface were being sent to their hereafter.

One of the sisters caught a spear in the chest. She did not survive long. Another had a bad wound on her leg from a spear. The wound was cleaned and bound. It would probably heal, leaving only a scar.

As the sun rose, the extent of the carnage became evident. The wounded were tended to first. Soaring Raven found Snow and Little Rose, concerned for them. He had a large gash in his left forearm. He had stopped a spear with his arm. Little Rose would not accept no for an answer. She cleaned and bound Soaring Raven's wound. She also cleaned and bound a gash on Snow's leg. He was not aware he had been cut. Guards were posted in case of another attack. Fortunately, few guards were needed in the daylight.

Graves were dug for the dead village people. The villagers all chanted together as many continued their work, asking the great spirits to accept the fallen. There was not time for all the traditional ceremonies and grieving. The dead Redface were laid in two rows. They were stripped of anything that was useable. Weapons were gathered up; they would be needed. Arrowheads that were stuck in flesh or bone of the Redface were dug out. Word soon spread that Snow and the Seven Sisters, at their original stand, had killed nine; and blood trails indicated that they had wounded at least three more. The final toll was not good. Forty-two Redface dead; thirty-nine village men, dead; six village women, dead; and five village men and three village women, seriously wounded. A war council was held; Snow was invited to attend.

Snow was asked how he and some women had killed so many.

Snow said, "We were in the right place, taking them by surprise. They fight different than us. We cannot stand up to them face-to-face. We must attack them like we hunt, not like they like to fight."

One of the old and wise war councilmen said, "Those that stood their ground fighting the Redface on their terms died. The Redface did not want to attack the line at the woods. They did not know we were running out of arrows, and the spears pointing at them were manned by women. The women archers on the hill were raining down death. The only weapon that they have that can be used against the archers is their throwing spear. They have to get close to use their throwing spears."

The decision was made; they did not have the men or other resources to withstand another attack. They would retreat to the River Village, carrying everything of value that they could carry. Food and other supplies that they could not carry would be burned or destroyed, as well as their lodges. They did not want to let their enemy profit from their attack.

Early the next morning, as the village burned, some of the women were lingering behind, especially those who had lost fathers, husbands, and sons. Snow and Little Rose's archers were to leave last, providing protection and helping the stragglers. In a display of anger that Snow did not know his people had, they brought fire to the crotches of the dead Redface, gouged out their eyes, and threw their gouged-out eyes into the fires. Snow wanted to stop the women from desecrating the bodies, though he also thought that they had their right to revenge. If the crazy woman was right, this would bring fear to the Redface that would find the corpses. Just maybe, they would not want their bodies in the hands of an enemy that would send them into their afterworld as blind women.

They were welcomed to the River Village as heroes who had fought a great battle in the name of all village people, not as refugees. The story of Snow and the Seven Sisters preceded them. They were pronounced as heroes by all. Every young woman and girl wanted to join the Seven Sisters. Snow observed a change in attitude; men were accepting women as fellow warriors.

The two war councils were merged. The war council of the Red Rock Village had lost three of its six members; they had died trying to face the Redface head-on with spears and war axes. Messengers were sent to the Lake Village to inform them of the situation, asking for weapons, mainly for arrows and spearheads.

Snow was asked to join the war council. This was a surprise to him; he was too young for such an honored position.

Snow told Little Rose, "The war council is to be made up of seasoned men who have shown that they can lead."

Little Rose said, "My husband, the people look up to you as a great warrior who had been tested in battle more than once, having shown his wisdom and bravery. People will listen to you and follow you. Accept who you are."

The war council was an emotional debate as to how to proceed. Snow just listened and tried to weigh all arguments fairly, tempered with his little experience. Some wanted to confront the Redface with spears and war axes, slugging it out in a brave stand of strength. Others wanted to conduct raids on the Redface's camps. Others were impressed with the success of the archers.

Soaring Raven said, "The Redface use a spear that they throw with a stick. I caught one with my arm. Most of our losses were from face-to-face battles, and other losses were from the spears that were thrown. We should consider learning to use these thrown spears." The Red Rock Village had been the largest of the villages. As such, it had the prestige with a leadership role. The Red Rock Village's chief had been made the combined war council's chief with the River Village chief as second in command.

After much debate, the chief said, "Snow, we have not heard from you. You have been successful. You and a group of women have killed many of our enemy. What do you think we should do?"

Snow said, "I believe that the Redface have more warriors than we do. We cannot win bashing at each other in the open. The Redface are not stupid. They will not group together in front of our archers, letting us stick arrows in them. Our archer will not win for us. We have seen that they are smart enough that they will not attack a line of many spears. We have to be smarter than they are, making them face all our strengths all at once. I believe we can only win by working together as one."

Snow received a round of "Uhs" in approval.

The consensus was that they would have to develop a way to fight that used all their strengths. Big Bear of the Red Rock Village was made chief of the warriors, Soaring Raven was made chief of the spears, and Snow was made chief of the archers. The war chief told his three assistant chiefs to develop their groups and try to find ways that they could work together to kill the Redface.

Snow and Little Rose no longer had their lodge to themselves. They had a woman and her three children sharing their lodge. Her husband had been killed in the battle for the Red Rock Village. She and her oldest, a twelve-year-old boy, wanted to become archers. Snow and Little Rose went for a walk to talk in private and to just enjoy holding each other's hand.

Little Rose asked, "How was your war council meeting?"

Snow answered, "They made me chief of the archers."

Little Rose said, "You make me proud that my husband is so respected."

Snow replied, "I am going to need an assistant. They will be the assistant chief of the archers."

Little Rose asked, "Do you know who you will chose?"

"Yes, you."

"You cannot choose me. I am a woman. A woman cannot be a chief."

"Who says a woman cannot be a chief? It is too late. You are the assistant chief of the archers. Accept who you are."

Little Rose answered, "Those are my words."

Snow replied, "Yes, good words."

In the coming days, many wanted to be archers, mostly women and boys who did not have the strength for other weapons. At first, bows were shared. There was not enough for everyone to have their own. They were organized into parties of five. An experienced archer was the leader. Each of the original sisters was a leader, as well as Snow was a leader. The sister that was wounded in the leg was healing. She took her place as a leader, walking with a stick. If the Redface gave them a couple more weeks, the archers would be able to shower their enemy with pain.

Several men complained to the chief about a woman as an assistant chief. The chief said the same to every man who complained, "Do you want the job? Chief of women and boys? For you, I will change the name to chief of women and boys."

Soaring Raven had twenty men and six strong women who practiced with the Redface throwing spear. They started to make their own. With experimentation, they found that with a lighter shank and a longer throwing fulcrum, they could make the spear travel farther with just as much penetrating power. They had a new weapon that improved their defenses. Soaring Raven also worked with the women who did not become archers to yield a hand spear. It was believed that the row of hand spears at the wood line at the Red Rock Village had discouraged the Redface from continuing their attack. If the enemy did not want to impale themselves, a quick thrust could be deadly. Two or three simultaneous thrusts against an opponent was hard to defend against. Spear of different length would let them line up in several lines with the longer spears in the back lines. This will make a wall of spear points. It was an invitation to go somewhere else.

It was noticed that on a couple of occasions, the Redface attacked in rows, shoulder to shoulder. Against an individual or a disorganized group, the results were good for the organized attack. The warriors were practicing using an organized attack. They even practiced giving a war cry in unison while swinging their weapons in unison. Observers concluded it was very intimidating. It was also noticed that some of the Redface wore heavy leather on their forearms and shoulders, and some had heavy leather hats protecting themselves. One of the dead Redface had three arrows in him; one of the arrows barely penetrated his heavy shoulder leather. A lot of the leather that was worn by the dead Redface were stripped from them and brought to the River Village. Soon there was a shortage of leather in the village. Old leather blankets and worn-out clothing was recycled. An old tunic or pair of pants that were doubled added some extra protection. There seemed to be a compromise; extra protection deceased agility and speed. Most of the women and girls were fashioning leather as protection. Some made hats that it was hard to tell if they were for protection or decoration, possibly both.

It had been eight days since the battle of Red Rock Village. A couple of armed patrols had been sent halfway to the Red Rock Village. There was no sign of the Redface. The moon was going into the new phase. Suspense of the unknown was taking a toll on the village people. Morale was falling, petty arguments were common, and there were a few fights.

Early one morning, Soaring Raven and Snow left to go up the mountain to look for signs of the Redface. They hoped that come dark they could see their fires. They climbed all day, keeping a good pace. They had not seen much game; only a couple of deer, a few rabbits, and a couple of spruce hens. Snow shot a rabbit for dinner. Near dark, they were well above the tree line but not near the top. They camped on a ridge going up the mountain, hoping to get a good view. They saw the fires of the Redface's main camp on the other side of the lake, though they could not see into the valley where the Red Rock Village was. They decided that they would walk along the mountain slope toward the Red Rock Village for a better view in the morning. It was good to be away from all the people, again hiking with his father, and being on the mountain. Dad's arm was healing. He stated that it did not work as good as it had before. He was exercising his arm, hoping it would get better.

The next morning, they headed out. The day was uneventful. Except they saw a herd of bighorn sheep. Toward late afternoon, they could clearly see the lake. They walked a little farther, hoping they would be able to see the village. The problem was they were rounding the mountain; the prairie could clearly be seen. They went as far as they could to get the best view of the village. To get a better view, they would have to go down. They did not want to take a chance of running into a Redface party. They were a long way from the village, so their view was not good. They could not see any activity. It looked like the lodges that they burned were not rebuilt. They would cold camp, no fire, so they could see where the Redface built their fires.

When it got dark, they could clearly see the campfires of the large camp on the other side of the lake. They could see several fires a long way out in the prairie. There were no fires near the village. There appeared to be a reflection off the canyon wall upstream from the Red Rock Village. They carefully retraced their path, back toward home. It was slow going in the dark. There was definitely a series of fires along the riverbank. One small fire looked to be an advanced party farther up the river.

Snow said, "Like the fire, we saw next to the lake before the attack on the Red Rock Village."

It was just downstream of a place they called the narrows about halfway from the River Village and the Red Rock Village. The canyon was narrow in that area. They cold camped where they were. In the morning, they headed home, making it by evening.

They immediately met with the war council. They concluded the Redface were on their territory in the narrow gorge. The village people knew the woods and mountains, the Redface did not. They were prairie people. They could go on the offensive with a quick surprise attack, then retreat, drawing the Redface into a trap. The deciding factor was that the battle would be away from the village. They needed to send out scouts to get an accurate position and an estimate of numbers.

Snow said, "The more scouts we send out, the more likely our plan will be revealed. Let them feel comfortable, not putting them on alert. I will go by myself."

Soaring Raven suggested, "We also need to send a small party above the tree line to keep track of their fires. They should report often. We should also post a guard on each side of the river and also scout the woods above the river to ensure that they do not try to sneak through the woods." There started to be a sliver of moon after sunset. It would not be long before there would be a bright moon.

Just as there was enough light to see, Snow headed out. He had pleaded with Little Rose to not follow him. He ended up making a deal with her. She would do the next scouting trip. He was going with only his knife for a weapon. Carrying a bow or spear made it more difficult to travel quietly through the thickets, where he wanted to go. His mission was information, not killing. He traveled parallel and up from the river far enough that he only got occasional looks at the water. Far enough away that detecting him from the path would be difficult. Snow knew these woods for he had often hunted in them since childhood. The first camp was where he believed it was the previous evening. They had not moved. It looked to have about a dozen warriors who seemed to be relaxing and sleeping, not in the least on guard. Snow had not come across any sign that would make him believe that they were exploring the woods. The second camp was where he thought it would be. The available firewood that was removed suggested that they were camped there for only a few days. Snow observed about forty to sixty warriors and the same number of women. A few of the women appeared to have leashes around their necks. There was what looked like two very young women, without any clothing, tied to the ground. There was some sign that a few of the warriors had explored up into the woods. Snow thought that he found a perfect place for an ambush between the two camps. Snow went higher to explore deeper into the woods. He heard something trying to move quietly through the woods. Snow lay in a small ravine and waited.

It was not long, and two scouts from the River Village were near. Snow softly said, "Can you two move a little quieter?" Of course, this startled the scouts.

Snow said, "I have scouted ahead. Maybe you can go a little higher, loop around even higher. Keep your eyes open. There is some sign that the Redface are scouting the woods in this area." Snow made it back to the village at sunset.

They had another war council. They had a report from a guard that a small party of three Redface had come near the village, scouting it. Per orders, they were made to believe that they were not detected. The plan was made. Twenty warriors, thirty archers, and ten spear-throwers would leave at the first hint of light. The rest of their fighters would remain in the village as a defense force if things went wrong. Little Rose left a little before everybody else as an advanced scout. Snow would lead. They would travel through the woods, trying to be quiet. At the place designated, they would divide into two groups. Snow gave a raven call. Little Rose soon appeared, giving an all clear. Little Rose led the archers, spear-throwers, and ten warriors to a spot that was known by her and Snow. Snow led the other ten warriors. Seven of the warriors were sent to the path upstream of the main camp to wait. The other three went with Snow to the camp with the majority of the Redface.

The greatest piece of luck happened to them. Near the camp was a small group of deer. Snow shot one of the deer in the buttocks, causing the deer to run. The warriors then started a ruckus, driving the deer toward the Redface camp. The three warriors broke onto the trail like they were a hunting party. The deer were panicked, running through the Redface camp. The warriors stood, looking at the camp like they were confused hunters. It did not take long for the Redface warriors to responded to the three hunters. The village hunters started to run down the trail pursued by about twelve Redface warriors. A short way down the trail were the other seven village warriors, walking in the direction of the camp. The ten formed a line, challenging the Redface. The Redface were not prepared for a battle. They sent one of their members back to their camp to bring all their warriors. After the runner entered the camp shouting that a battle had started and some of their warriors needed help, Snow stepped out onto the trail, unleashing a volley of two arrows into two of the warriors' chests in their camp. Snow then turned and ran down the trail. The skirmish of the warriors did not last long. One of the village warriors and one of the Redface warriors were killed. Blood had been drawn. The village warriors retreated to a position a little farther up the trail to a point where the trail was narrow between the river that ran up against a cliff and a low cliff, meeting up with their fellow warriors. The river was narrow here, running fast and deep. The village warriors formed a blocking unit. They were formable in the narrow gap. The Redface decided to wait for reinforcements. It did not take long until most all the Redface warriors arrived, charging the village warriors. The hidden archers and spear-throwers rained death down on the Redface. Soon those still standing tried to retreat as more arrows rained down. They had no cover. Forty-seven Redface warriors lay dead or dying. No mercy was shown.

A group of ten spear-throwing warriors and ten archers were to come from the village to eradicate the forward camp. Eight of

Snow's warriors were to head back toward the village to keep the Redface from the forward camp from escaping. Ideally, they wanted no witnesses to tell the other Redface of their enemy's resourcefulness. Through the woods, Snow led the archers to the Redface's main camp. It was now the second part of their plan. The remaining village warriors and spear-throwers headed down the path toward the main Redface camp at a leisurely pace. Little Rose took half of the archers to the other side of the camp to cut off any escape. Snow positioned his archers near the camp. When the warriors and spear throwers arrived the archers moved closer shooting arrows into anything that appeared to have a weapon as the warriors formed a line marching into the camp with the spear throwers flanking them. It did not take long. They were not prepared to fend off an attack. Some of the warriors came out of their flimsy hide-covered shelters with no clothing on. Women were screaming, some in fear and some rejoicing being rescued. A couple of women were shot, trying to yield weapons and a few trying to escape. The women who were obvious slaves were freed, helping tie up the women who were not. One Redface man was found lying in his hut. He appeared to be only partially conscious. He was tied up. He would be taken back to the village for questioning, along with the women prisoners. Two of the rescued women were from the fish camp. They were village people.

They picked up what they could carry, especially weapons and leather armor; then they headed back to the village. Tomorrow, people would return to take what was left that was of some use. The skin shelters might be of some use. The forward camp had been surprised; all the warriors were killed. Upon returning to the village, the results were summed up. Sixty-one Redface warriors were killed and one taken prisoner. Four Redface women were killed. Twenty-four slaves freed, five were pregnant. Fifteen Redface women were taken prisoner. Three village warriors were killed, two village warriors were injured, and no archers or spear-throwers were injured. That night, there would be a celebration in the village.

The Redface warrior prisoner refused to talk. The two village women who were rescued from slavery acted as interpreters. Snow was observing; he wanted information. The crazy old woman showed up. Without saying a word she reached under Snow's tunic taking his knife. Everyone had heard the rumor that Snow carried a special knife. The fact that the crazy old woman would dare reach under Snow's tunic then brandish his knife made all step back; this was not appropriate or expected. The look of the knife brought awe to all. These were strange times. The crazy old woman went to the prisoner, brandishing the knife to his face. The Redface warrior looked at the knife with an expression of terror. The crazy old woman licked the backside of the knife with her tongue, spat three times into the face of the Redface warrior, held the knife vertically against the prisoner's nose, slightly drawing it down, drawing drips of blood from the cut. The Redface man's eyes widened and crossed, trying to see the knife. The crazy woman whispered something in his ear. The brave warrior started to weep. The crazy old woman returned to Snow, handing him the knife, hilt first; and in a quiet, quivering voice, said, "He will talk now." Talk, he did. The sight of the knife, the ceremony, or whatever was told to him brought great fear to him. The Redface that were killed were the forward party sent to establish a camp and scout. Many more Redface were coming. The Redface feared the valley people. They sent their warriors to the heavens as blind women. It would be better to be burned and destroyed forever. The rescued slaves provided more information of the customs and culture of the Redface. The Redface believed that they were chosen to rule the world, and anyone not a Redface man was of no value. They were made to be used or killed by the Redface men. Slaves that were not good at providing nooky and work were used as targets to practice killing. It was concluded that for the Redface society to survive they had to conquer, taking slaves. Boy babies were a blessing; girl babies were a burden. They had to be fed until they got big enough to be of any use—for labor, for nooky, and to bear children.

A group of people were sent to salvage what was of value at the Redface camps. A group of older women insisted on going and helping. All knew what their intentions were; none questioned their actions. Openly, nobody condoned their actions; though all secretly admired them. Snow and Little Rose in private agreed it was horrible that an effective weapon against brutality and cruelty was more brutality and cruelty to instill fear. The stories told by the rescued slaves hardened the hearts and strengthened the resolve of the village people. There came a report from the lookouts up the side of the mountain. More fires were seen along the river near the Red Rock Village. More Redface were coming. It was concluded that they would not fall for the same trap again. It was possible that some had escaped. Also, the demise of their fellow Redface would be suspicious.

The next morning, the Redface warrior prisoner was found with his throat slit, with his privates removed, and with no eyes. Nobody took credit; nobody asked. The Redface women were rebellious at first, wanting revenge. In a few days, seeing the village women carrying weapons and being trained to use them, as well as seeing that they were treated with respect, not beaten, or abused, they started to change their attitude. Given a choice of remaining bound or helping, they chose helping. A controversial decision was made. There were two choices: make the Redface women slaves or give them their freedom. They were given their freedom. They were told that there was a Redface camp a day's walk down the trail. They were free to go, or they could stay. If they stayed, they would be expected to follow the village people's rules and help with the work. They all chose to stay. One morning, one of the Redface women was found viciously beaten. Upon questioning, she would only say that it was appropriate and expected. She appreciated that she was still alive. There was a rumor that the woman who got the beating was unusually cruel to the slaves, often doing the dirty work for a Redface chief. The villager's fear of the Redface was turning into hatred.

Snow had been given credit for the plan that brought about the demise of the Redface camps. The more that he told people that he just used other's ideas, the more respect he seemed to get. The war council gave Snow a job he did not want. He was to come up with a plan to stop the new threat. Snow felt overwhelmed. The responsibility was a burden he did not want. Snow went to his father, asking for advice.

Soaring Raven said, "I will help you in any way I can, though I have no idea of what can be done. I believe that the only way we will permanently stop the Redface is instill them with so much fear that they will take their evil elseward." This left Snow even more unsettled. *Fear* and *evil* were bad words.

Next, it was the person that knew him better than he felt he knew himself, Little Rose. Snow and Little Rose's relationship grew out of an unlikely match of people. Their strength was their faith and love for each other. They each trusted the other more than they trusted themselves. They could communicate with a look or gesture. Although they did not always agree, they could come to an agreement. Each made the other stronger and complete.

Little Rose asked Snow, "Can we find another valley that is peaceful, like our ancestors did, then live in peace for several generations?"

Snow replied, "If that is what you want, I will go with you and look."

Little Rose said, "That is my selfish dream. Neither of us can abandon our people."

Snow said, "I do not know what to do. I have no ideas."

Little Rose replied, "Look for a weakness. Ask the women who were their slaves and wives. Women know their men."

Snow took Little Rose with him. She was respected by the other women. She had a reputation of being a woman's woman who did not let men intimidate her but loved her man completely. Snow knew. He got criticism for not being able to control his wife, setting a bad example.

The two ex-slave women who were villagers were asked to help. The Redface women were learning the new language; still, communication was difficult. The Redface women felt honored that these two heroes would come asking for their advice. There was a lot of information, some confusing and some contradictory. One thing that became apparent was that women were of no consideration and were of no consequence to the Redface. A Redface man was brave and strong; a woman was nothing. The Redface woman who was beaten said, "Beating or killing a Redface woman means nothing, they are used to it, showing a woman respect has value. Thank you for letting me stay here. I will accept the beatings I have earned. I never deserved the beatings I received from my husband."

They were told that the Redface liked to have bonfires, tell stories, chew crazy leaves until late at night, then sleep a long time when they were not warring.

Snow said, "They consider that women have no value. When they conquer a people, they kill all the men, keeping the women. Women are easy to come by as long as they can conquer other people."

Little Rose responded, "What if the Redface women knew that women were killing their men and sparing their women, treating the women with respect?"

Snow answered, "Sounds like you want to confuse them. You sure have confused me."

Little Rose said, "With all the fires we see on the prairie, we cannot kill all the Redface. But if we rescue their women, they will eventually run out of women. Some of the women will turn on them. No women, no Redface. Attack their camps. Rescue the women."

Snow said, "That makes sense to me. Why fight at our village. Fight at their camps."

Little Rose asked, "There are a lot more women than men here. Most women want a man. A lot of men are taking a second wife. Do you want a second wife?

Snow answered, "I definitely do not want a second wife; you are more wife than I can handle."

Fifteen warriors, nine archers, along with eight boys, who were rock throwers aged about ten to twelve, came from the Lake Village to help defend the valley from the Redface. With them they brought many spear and arrowheads. They also brought a lot of unworked flint. These were valuable gifts; flint was hard to find. The traders had taken a Redface throwing spear to the Lake Village. A young man called Setting Owl of the Lake Village who spend all his time fiddling with things remade the throwing spear. When he demonstrated his improved throwing spear the warriors were impressed. Their spears were smaller than those of the River Village spear-throwers. Their fulcrums were equipped with a leather thong that gripped the end of the spear. A warrior could carry several throwing spears, along with a fulcrum for launching them. They demonstrated their accuracy and distance that the spear could be thrown. All were impressed. Soon many were being trained and practicing with this improved weapon. The rock throwers also were impressive; they had two leather thongs that were attached to a shallow leather basket that they placed a rock in. They swung it around, then at the appropriate moment, released one thong, throwing the rock. All agreed that they would not want to be hit with one of the rocks. It was basically a child's toy turned into a weapon. The archers also showed proficiency. Each archer and rock thrower also carried in their sash a light war ax with a long handle. A demonstration of these war axes convinced all archers and spear-throwers that they wanted one. It seemed that everyone in the village wanted to be a soldier. The rescued slave women became archers or spear-throwers. Even a few of the Redface women swore allegiance, becoming a part of the defense. The peaceful people of three villages united to become an impressive army dedicated to the destruction of their enemy.

Every evening, the moon got higher in the evening sky. Snow and Little Rose spent a lot of their time spying on the enemy. They watched the Redface train and practice. The Redface appeared to have one tactic. Attack with overwhelming numbers spreading terror, routing their prey from their villages. They appeared to have four weapons: war ax, war club, throwing spear, and knife. They did not seem to be concerned with the security of their camps. They posted no guards. Snow concluded that they arrogantly believed that no one would dare attack them. Snow and Little Rose also witnessed the brutality that they used against their women. The Redface demanded total obedience from their women, slave or wife. This was enforced with brutal cruelty. It was often hard to tell the difference from a slave and a wife. Every few days, the Redface moved their two camps closer to the village. Every few days, the Redface would send out a party of three to check on their intended target. Per orders, the village tried to put on an appearance of vulnerability. All training was on the far side of the village. The Redface seemed to not like to climb up the hillsides, preferring the paths. The Redface spies would not be challenged, letting them think that they were undetected. The Redface spies were shown a peaceful village, giving them the opinion they were large in number against a peaceful, unprepared village—an easy prize. When the Redface reached the site where many of their fellow warriors were laid out to display their lack of eyes and privates, they built several large fires, burning the corpses. The horrible smell filled the valley. The Redface were sending their companions into oblivion; better than spending eternity as blind women.

CHAPTER 4

The village army was divided into four groups; each group had a variety of warriors, archers, and spear-throwers. The anticipation was the hardest thing. The sun had set; the scout arrived, saying that the Redface were settling into camp for the night with large bonfires. They were not preparing for battle. The village people did not want to start an attack to find that the Redface were moving to attack their village. The first group departed under moonlight, guided by guards that were dispersed in the woods. This group, led by Snow, would travel to the far side of the main Redface camp through the woods, trying to not be detected. An hour later, the second group left, led by Soaring Raven; they would attack directly into the center of the camp. Then the third group departed, led by Big Bear; they would drop down onto the path between the Redface forward camp and the main camp. A fourth small group would head down the path at sunrise, blocking the forward camp from entering the village. All made it to their positions while they still had moonlight. The moon soon set; this was the time that all were to rest, preparing for their attack. As daylight broke, they all started to move in, trying to not be detected. The attack was to be exactly when the sun broke over the mountain.

The Redface camp was stretched along the riverbank; in the early morning light, the camp was surrounded by the village warriors with their throwing spears ready. They were backed up by archers with arrows nocked and ready. Intermixed were spear-throwers. Also there was a group of boys with rocks ready in their slings. The sun broke over the mountain, casting its rays of light over the whole scene. Nothing happened; the camp was asleep. The heavy breathing of the nervous soldiers could be heard along with the water talking as it went its way downstream. An eerie silence before the storm. A man stepped from his tent; he started to urinate. In rapid succession, he was struck by at least six arrows. He let out a scream of pain. People started to emerge from their tents to be quickly struck with arrows. The village people started to move closer. Most of the Redface warriors did not have their leather armor on or their weapons in hand. Pandemonium soon broke out. Arrows, spears, and rocks flew; then a few of the Redface warriors started charging with their axes; they were quickly cut down. Some of the village warriors lined up, bashing their way forward through the camp. Soon there was no sign of any kind of order; it became a brawl. A few had tried to escape the slaughter; they were quickly dispatched with arrows. Some dove into the river to be struck with arrows by the archers assigned to the downstream riverbank. As there were few standing enemy targets, the archers and spear-throwers moved in with their war axes, bashing the skulls of the men who still moved or groaned. Eventually, the only thing to be heard were the screams and pleading of women and a few children. Every Redface man had been mercilessly killed.

The women and children were herded into a clearing upstream and told to sit quietly. The ex-slaves and rescued Redface women from the previous battle went among the captured women and children, tending to their wounds and trying to explained that they would not be harmed if they cooperated and caused no trouble. One slave woman was found near death with her eyes gouged out. Five village warriors and one woman archer had been killed. Eight villager warriors and two women archers had been seriously injured. There were many minor injuries; no one counted them. Eighty-two Redface warriors were counted dead; the downstream archers claimed three more that were washed downriver. Twenty-seven Redface women and two slaves, as well as eleven children, were killed. Some were unintentional casualties; others had tried to put up a fight. The older boys seemed to think themselves warriors.

Big Bear, Soaring Raven, and Snow stood together, looking at the carnage.

Snow stated, "This is a great victory for the village people, why do I feel so empty?"

Soaring Raven stated, "It is a great victory for our people, though, it would have been better if the Redface had not came, causing all this death."

Big Bear lamented, "There will be much celebrating in the village tonight. The only thing worth celebrating is that few of our people died."

The Redface advanced camp was taken with the loss of three village people, two of which were women who enthusiastically charged with spears. They were surprised and fell mainly to arrows and spears. Nine more Redface went to eternity as blind women.

Before the celebration in the River Village, the shaman asked all to be quiet in respect. He then asked the great spirits and their ancestors to accept all the slain village people into their eternal village.

The celebration in the River Village was one of joy. They had not been killed or enslaved. There was not a lot of food to go around. There were more mouths to feed, and everyone had been working, preparing for war. Few went fishing, hunting, and gathering. Reports came that there were no fires seen along the river trail. The newly freed slaves seemed to not know what to do; they were not used to freedom. The Redface women and children were not bound. They were confused. After seeing the carnage, they did not want to do anything other than what they were told to do. They were the prisoners of people that killed all that resisted. After seeing the village women's deadly accuracy with a bow and arrow, then bashing the heads of the men with their war ax, the captured women feared all the villagers, including the women. The immediate threat being eliminated, tomorrow Snow was going fishing.

Early next morning, Snow went fishing to his special spot. It was not long until he had several nice fish lying in the grass. Something was tickling his ear. He swatted it. It was a blade of grass. Snow pretended to not be concerned. When he felt the tickle again, he quickly turned, then sprung, catching Little Rose in his right arm. It was a wrestling match. Eventually, Little Rose let herself be overcome. They had been sharing their lodge and were busy. It was a special occasion, sharing a closeness together. After an extended time in each other's arms, they both went back to fishing. By midafternoon they had a basketful of fish. Returning to the village, Snow dropped one nice fish, that would fill a belly, in front of the crazy old woman's hut.

Snow told Little Rose, "Today was a good day. For a while, I felt that things were good again."

Little Rose said, "I know that it is not easy for you. You do set an example for many. You make our people stronger."

Snow replied, "You set an even greater example. Women admire you, and men respect you."

In the village, Snow asked who wanted fish. He was directed to an area that was set up with Redface tents. The women from the Redface camp were setting up a camp for themselves and their children. Snow and Little Rose were welcomed and praised for bringing them fish. The woman who was blinded was sitting. Someone had brought her a bundle of reeds. She was weaving a basket. When one of the previously freed slaves was asked of her remarkable recovery, they were told she needed two things—food and hope. Talking to her, it was found out that she had been taken as a prisoner from the Red Rock fishing camp.

The blind woman told them, "My husband, who was killed, was a good fisherman. I wove fishnets and baskets for his fish. The night that I was captured, I tried to resist a Redface's advances. As an example, he had me held down, then he gouged my eyes out. He laughed when he gouged my eyes out. He enjoyed my screams. Then he had his way with me. It is of some comfort that he will be a blind woman for eternity like I am."

Snow told the woman, "As a villager, when your time comes, you will be accepted into our eternal village where you will rejoin your husband, whole and eternally healthy. Our ancestors have prepared a much different place than the Redface ancestors."

The next day, Snow and Little Rose went hunting. They climbed up to near the tree line. They shot a rabbit, stopping to cook it for lunch. Again, they reaffirmed their closeness, enjoying each other. Returning to the village, Little Rose shot a nice buck that was in velvet. Snow bagged two rabbits. The village would have some fresh meat tonight. Part of their game fed the women who were from the Redface camp.

Again, the captured women were shown respect and given food. It appeared that the ex-slaves and Redface women were working together. Later, Little Rose asked one of the previously freed slaves why they seemed to be working in harmony.

An ex-slave said, "The ex-slaves and warrior widows have a lot in common. Working together would make them stronger. If they were strong, no evil man could ever brutalize them again. They could be free women, raising their children in freedom."

That evening, Snow and Little Rose went for a walk along the river; they were holding hands.

Little Rose said, "I think those women, whether ex-slaves or ex-wives, knowing that they have freedom, will fight hard to keep it. They will be great allies."

Snow asked, "How do we tell the Redface that their women want to kill them, then making blind women out of them for eternity?"

Little Rose answered, "Word will get around. That is the way things are."

The next several days, Snow and Little Rose went hunting and fishing. It started to feel like life was good, flowing in peace and harmony with their world. They tried hard to quiet the memories of the horrible battles that they had witnessed and participated in. Little things seemed sweeter: the call of the songbirds, the talking of the water as it went on its journey down the river, the touches that they shared, the smiles and greetings of their fellow villagers, and the children play the games that led to maturity. All seemed to have the sweet sound of peace and harmony.

From the freed slaves and Redface widows, they learned of other tribes of people. Some from far away that lived in hills on the other side of the prairie. All were enemies of the Redface. Two freed slaves that were sisters told of how their entire tribe was destroyed. They had lived along a river far away, near mountains that could not be seen from here. They were from the other side of the prairie; many, many days' walk.

Snow and Little Rose could not deny that the threat still existed. They knew that it was just a matter of time until the Redface would again attack. The Redface's society required new slaves to maintain their way of life. The war council maintained a small group that kept a lookout on the mountain. Their reports said that the Redface camp on the other side of the Red Rock Village Lake was not as large as it was, and no fires were seen that were any closer. Snow and Little Rose decided to take advantage of the pause in hostilities and the pleasant summer weather to do some exploring. Nobody knew of anyone to ever climbing the mountains on the south side of the river. They wondered if beyond the peaks there was another valley. What did the prairie look like from there? Were the animals different there? Were there other people living there? They had many questions.

CHAPTER 5

Snow and Little Rose would each carry their bows. Snow would carry a large hand spear in case they could not avoid a confrontation with a bear. Little Rose would carry one of the smaller throwing spears. They each carried some dried fruit, meat, and fish, as well as herbs and medicine. They also carried one of the small tents that was made by the Redface women. They went across the river on a large tree that had fallen across the river, using it as a bridge. The valley side was steeper on this side of the river. The trees were smaller and less dense. This side of the valley got less sun. In the winter, this side was always in the shade of the mountains. By midday they were above the tree line; they stopped to take a break. From where they were, the valley, river, and their village looked beautiful and peaceful. From their position, they had a good view of their valley. They could see most of the length of the valley, especially toward the Red Rock Village. They could see the Red Rock Cliff.

Snow said, "This would be a good position for a lookout. They could signal with a fire that could be seen in the village."

By early evening, their leg muscles were complaining. They found a nice flat spot where they could camp. They had not seen a lot of game. Little Rose shot a spruce hen that they would share for dinner. There was only brush for a fire. Their fire would do for cooking, though it required being continuously tended.

Little Rose said, "Look, our village fires can be seen. If they look up, they will see our fire."

By midday the next day, they were climbing on bare rock. They were trying to go to a split between the mountains. There was no game or anything to burn, just bare rock. By midafternoon they needed to use their hands to continue. Finding a small ledge, they sat, taking a break. The view of the prairie looked hazy. The view of their valley was spectacular. From here it looked small; it did not look real. Looking across, it looked like they were as high as the pass they had been in when they climbed to see the prairie. It was getting hard to keep their breath; they both were breathing hard. They agreed that they would stop and camp when they found a large enough flat spot. A couple of hours later, they were working their way up a steep ravine, then to their surprise, they found themselves in a narrow crack. They could see through to other mountains at a distance. They moved enough rocks to sleep with some comfort. There was no room to set up their tent. It was so narrow that they could not sleep side by side. After a little fun debating, it was decided if it got cold, Little Rose would sleep on top of Snow. If it got really cold, Snow would sleep on top. They were so tired that this little bit of verbal jousting called the end to their day. At least they would not worry about falling down; they were jammed in tight.

In the morning, they were sitting on a small flat area overlooking a valley that did not look much different than their valley. The problem was that there was almost a vertical cliff in front of them. The steepness decreased a little way down. Without a rope, they did not think that they could safely descend. There was a narrow ledge going to their left. As she usually did, Little Rose gave Snow great concern. She went along the ledge. The ledge curved away so Snow could not see her. Snow had no choice other than to sit, trying to patiently wait.

It was not long until he heard Little Rose's voice from below him. "Slide our gear down. It looks good from here."

Snow did as he was told. He did not feel brave when he went on the ledge. It was not far to a spot that had some grooves, making handholds so he could get down. It was not far down where the slope became easier, where they could descend using their feet and hands. They started to see some grasses and mosses. They saw a herd of bighorn sheep. These animals were wonderful to watch. They could balance on slivers of rock then bound to a narrow ledge. By early evening, they made it to the tree line. They shot a spruce hen and a rabbit. Here there was plenty of wood for a fire. This was a comfortable camp compared to the last two they had. Near dark, Snow and Little Rose went on top of a rock outcropping to look for fires. There was a couple of fires down below. Now there were more questions. The biggest question was, Whose fires?

The decision was easy. Go down to see who these people were. By midafternoon they were near a village. They moved stealthily toward the village. What if they were Redface? A couple of boys walked by them. They were hunting, although they were more interested in insulting each other the way boys did. Their language was almost the same as theirs. They pronounced some words differently.

Little Rose stood up, saying, "Hey, boys, is there any game around here?" The boys turned around. The expression on their faces said it all.

Snow stood, saying, "Do not let her scare you. She likes to scare boys."

One of the boys asked, "Who are you?"

"I am Snow. This is Little Rose, my wife. We came over the mountain." He pointed toward the mountain. "Will you take us to your village and introduce us?"

One of the boys replied, "Okay, follow us."

Little Rose asked, "What kind of game do you have around here?"

The boy replied, "Deer, elk, rabbit, squirrel, and birds."

Little Rose asked, "Mind if I take a rabbit if I see one?"

The boy said, "Sure."

Little Rose knocked an arrow, drew, letting the arrow fly. She walked over picking up a rabbit.

One of the boys exclaimed, "Wow."

Little Rose said, "Dinner."

The other boy said, "I never seen him." The boys led them to the village. It was similar to their village, only a little smaller. The few women working on their chores stopped what they were doing, staring at the strangers. Soon they were approached by three men.

One of the boys said, “Chief, this is Snow and his wife, Little something.”

The chief said, “Welcome to our village. We do not get visitors. We do not know what to do.”

Snow answered, “We are from the River Village that is in the valley that is on the other side of the mountains. We come in peace and friendship. My wife, Little Rose, and I are pleased to meet you and your people.”

The chief asked, “Did you walk over the mountains.”

Snow replied, “Yes, it took us three sleeps.”

The chief said, “Please enjoy our village, rest. We will feast tonight.”

Snow replied, “Thank you for your hospitality.”

The two boys appointed themselves as Snow’s and Little Rose’s personal guides. They must have been introduced to twenty people. Taken down to their river, they were told of the fish that could be caught and how they caught them. Snow got the boys to sit with him and Little Rose on the riverbank. Snow asked where their people came from and of their legends. Their legends were similar to those of the village people. Their home was the prairie. They were driven to this valley by the evil Redface people. Their language and customs were similar; these people were the cousins of the village people. It was not long until they were surrounded by children and young adults. Their curiosity was obvious. Snow and Little Rose answered all their questions except one. They asked if they had seen the Redface. Snow wanted to address this issue with their council. All the girls were very interested in Little Rose’s bow. Little Rose gave them a lesson in archery. Most did not have the strength to draw her bow.

She told them, “If you are nice to your fathers and mothers and asked nice, maybe your fathers will make you your own bow.” Her throwing spear got a lot of interest from the older boys. She told them that later she would show them how it worked.

By early evening, Snow was invited to the council with the men of the tribe. After the formal greetings, Snow asked if he could speak to the council. He told of his people’s legends, saying that they were cousins. He told of his people’s valley and how it was like their valley.

Then he told how their village was attacked by the Redface and of people dying. He told of the brutality by Redface toward women and their unrelenting need to kill all men who were not Redface. He told how many Redface women and slaves had been rescued and how the wives of the Redface wanted to be free of their abusive husbands. Snow warned them that if the Redface knew of them, they would attack, kill all the men, then enslave their women. Snow stated that their women and even older children had learned to use weapons. Without them they would have lost in battle.

One man asked, “What proof do you have of these things you spoke of.”

Snow answered, “I only have my words. I hope you are not faced with the proof. Seeing the proof will probably mean the deaths of many.”

Snow was informed that their people had another village, the Village of Falling Waters. It was downstream along the river. The prairie could be seen from there. He was told he should go there and tell their council what he had told them. When they were ready to leave, the chief would send a guide with them to introduce them.

Their hosts built a bonfire with a feast of good food. These people also enjoyed dancing around the fire as couples. A couple of young ladies asked Little Rose if Snow had brought her the hide and antlers of a great antlered elk. That was the way a man asked a woman to bond with him in their tribe. Little Rose told that Snow had brought her the hide of a bear. That was the way their tribe tested a man. When asked how big was the bear, Little Rose said, “A very big bear.” These people’s traditions were similar but a little different. Their values were the same. The girls got Little Rose and Snow to dance around the fire together. They were not very good at it. It was their first time dancing together. Their River Village did not have men and women dancing together. They agreed that they would take dancing together around the fire back to their village.

The next day, Little Rose demonstrated her throwing spear. Snow showed the boys how to make a sling, showing them how to throw a rock. A lot of the men and older boys were interested in the throwing spear. They borrowed Little Rose’s spear and fulcrum, copy it, making their own. Two girls showed up with their own bows. They said that they had to promise their fathers they would work hard and mind their mothers. Snow noticed that their arrows and spearheads were made from a gray flint of exceptional quality. It was found out that they had a large vein of it. He also found out that they had a shortage of salt. Both he and Little Rose brought some salt with them. They gave it to the people. It was obvious that trade should be established between their two tribes. They stayed one more day. They had made some new friends. All had learned new things.

The Village of Falling Waters was smaller than the Valley Village. They were greeted with enthusiasm; the village knew that guests were coming. Everyone seemed to know all about them. They wanted to have a demonstration of the throwing spear and of the use of a sling. Little Rose was asked many questions about archery. Some of the young ladies set up a target, asking Little Rose demonstrate her skills. The ones that could pull her bow got to try to hit the target. One girl of about ten came with her own bow. Little Rose gave her instructions. After a few tries, she was hitting the center of the target. The ten-year-old lent her bow to the other girl who wanted a try. By evening, there was the start of a team of girl archers.

Snow gave a report to the Village of Falling Waters council of the possible threat of the Redface. They asked Snow if he would climb partway up their mountain to show them the fires on the prairie. They arranged that the next afternoon Snow would go up with a party of their men to a place where they could observe the prairie. They would spend the night.

The next morning, Snow was shown how their river flowed between the mountains, down into many small ponds, then onto the prairie. The path to the prairie was narrow next to the rapid water of the river between two rock faces. Snow was told that when the flow of water was great, the path could not be used, isolating the valley.

In the afternoon, Snow left with a small party of the Village of Falling Waters' men. They did not want Little Rose going with them. They expressed their concerns that she was a woman who did not have the strength or courage to climb. Snow pointed to the high mountains, saying, "Little Rose came into this valley with me over those mountains. She is a better mountain climber than I."

The men decided that Little Rose could accompany them. The path was steep, with many places that were narrow where it would be easy to slip. A person could easily fall off the high cliff. The path went around the mountain toward the north, continually getting higher. Eventually, they could go no further, for there was only a cliff in front of them. From there, they could look out over the prairie. They could see the lake and part of the Red Rock Cliff that was near the Red Rock Village. The great river could be seen snaking its way through the prairie. Nothing could be seen of the Redface. They watched the sun set over another line of mountains much farther away.

Little Rose said, "Our world is bigger than I ever thought. Does it go on forever?"

Snow replied, "I do not think it makes any difference. We will never be able to walk to its edge."

None of the men who came with them knew of anyone to ever spend the night up here. Few came up here. Some came to think and talk to their ancestors.

As dark came, the fires of the Redface camp beyond the Red Rock Lake could be seen, as well as many more fires spread across the prairie. Several small campfires were spotted near what was believed to be on the path from the prairie to the Village of Falling Waters.

Upon returning to the Village of Falling Waters the next morning, a council was called. Snow was asked to join. The council called for a war council. Snow was asked to join their war council. Snow refused, saying he needed to get back to his valley. Snow did agree to stay a few days to advise their war council.

A messenger was sent to the Valley Village, asking for help. A position partway up the trail on the mountain was found where a spotter could be positioned every night to watch the prairie fires near the approach to the Village of Falling Waters. The people of the village were prepared for war. Weapons were made, and food were stored in preparation. Little Rose trained the women and girls in archery and the use of the throwing and handheld spears. The men practiced and trained in throwing spears and war axes. Rocks were balanced on the cliff over the path, ready to be rolled off onto the path. Positions for the archers and spear-throwers were found.

Snow advised, “The Redface are not fools. They will not attack a position that they know is well defended. They like to attack using surprise.”

Reports came that the fires were getting larger and greater in numbers. The moon was waxing, soon to be full. Care was taken to conceal their defenses. They had hiding places for their archers and spear-throwers near their defense positions. Many came from the Valley Village to help defend their valley.

Snow warned that they would send in scouts, probably three men, the nights before they attacked. Following Snow’s advice, the Redface scouts were shown a sleepy unarmed village. The Redface sent scouts two night in a row. The moon was nearing full. All was prepared; all waited in anticipation and fear. The young children, pregnant women, and women with nursing children had been moved to the Valley Village.

Little Rose told the women archers, “The hardest part was waiting. Once a battle began, their blood would run hot. Their fear would be forgotten. Follow your training. Be patient. Wait for the signal to attack.”

Few were sleeping soundly in their lodges. Many had taken to sleeping in the day. They were ready. The call of an owl was heard. As planned, all defender went quietly to their positions. Little Rose was in a position where she could see most of the path. Little Rose would call the archers to their firing positions when most of the Redface were on the path, starting their attack.

What looked like six Redface slowly moved up the path. They were not stopped. When they approached what looked to them as a sleepy village, one of them called a crow call. They sat down, waiting in the shadows. The Redface stared to ascend the path in great numbers. When the Redface neared the top of the path, Little Rose gave a cricket sound. Many crickets could be heard just before arrows were raining down on the Redface. At the bottom of the path, rocks rained down, crushing the Redface that were at the end of the line. The bottom of the path was littered with bodies and rocks, making a retreat difficult. Village warriors overwhelmed the six Redface that were near the village, then they headed to the top of the path, making a line of spears and flaying battle axes. Arrows and spears continued to reign down at anything that moved on the path. A few tried to escape back over their fellow dead Redface and the rocks. More rocks came down. A small group of archers shot arrows at the few that tried to retreat. It was not long till village warriors went down the path, completing the job that they had started.

As the sun rose, there seemed to be an eerie quiet over the valley. Forty-four Redface lay dead, two village warriors were injured, their wounds would heal. The Redface were stripped then thrown into the river. Neither Snow nor Little Rose had said anything of the mutilations, so there was none. Most all rocks and bodies being cleared the villagers descended, wanting to complete the destruction of the Redface. Snow and Little Rose were hesitant in continuing their attack, not knowing how many Redface were in their camp. They went with the villagers.

The war chief had the Redface camp surrounded. They moved in, finding mainly women and a few children. The few Redface warriors that remained put up a futile fight till death. Some of the older boys also would not surrender; one boy impaled himself on a spear rather than surrender. Nineteen Redface women were captured, fourteen slave women were freed, two had their eyes gouged out. There were about twenty children of varying ages.

The problem was what to do with thirty-something women and twenty-something children. A couple of the slaves were able to translate; some of the slaves were from tribes that had been destroyed at the far side of the prairie. Snow had asked the other men about taking slaves. The village people did not take slaves. It was against their beliefs. Little Rose insisted that she be able to talk to the assembled women. She tried to explain to them through the interpreters their situation. It was difficult for some of them to understand that they would not be slaves. They were free women to decide their own fate, as long as they treated the village people with respect. Some of these women had never been given the choice of choosing their own destiny. They were always controlled by their fathers, husbands, masters, or elders—always a male. Now there were no males of their tribe to control them. The women were given the opportunity to say their peace.

Most sat mute; one asked Little Rose, "What would you do?"

Little Rose answered, "I am fortunate. I do not have to face your decision. I am blessed with a good husband that I follow. He is brave, strong, and wise. He also asks my advice, makes his decisions asking me what I think, and I follow him. I follow him by my choice. You all must make your own choice."

Little Rose left them to talk among themselves.

The war chief and his council decided to let the women make their own choice. They would not harm women or children. They believed that if they did evil, their ancestors would let them lie in their graves forever to ponder their evil ways.

All the slave women and twelve of the Redface women wanted to stay with the village people. The other Redface women wanted to go and be with their own tribe. The Redface women, leaving, asked if they could take a few weapons to protect themselves. They were permitted to take a few weapons. They were told to not return with more men and to find peace in their hearts. One of the departing Redface women told Little Rose, "If our women can be strong like you and the other women of your tribe, maybe we can teach our men to respect us. If they cannot learn respect, then they need to learn fear."

The ex-slave women and some of the wives gouged out the eyes, burned them, and burned the privates of the few dead Redface warriors in the camp, demonstrating their hatred toward the Redface men.

Snow and Little Rose decided to head for home from where they were. They had fulfilled what they wanted to do. They knew what was over the mountains. They had made new friends and allies. They had helped prepare and warned their cousins of the threat. They had helped them vanquish more Redface and found another source of flint that could be traded for with salt. The journey was a success. As they were saying their goodbyes, two of the young freed slave women asked if they could go with them. Neither Snow nor

Little Rose could say no. All four of them carried a load of flint. The two women used a drag to take their possessions.

From where they were, they could see the Red Rock Cliff off in the distance. They guessed it was a day's walk. It was midafternoon. They were tired. They had been up all night. In a couple of hours, they found a nice place to camp near a small stream. They started to cold camp, not wanting to show their position to any possible enemy on the prairie. It was not long until Snow and Little Rose found that there were a lot they could learn from their traveling companions. They were raised on the prairie, buffalo hunting, buffalo hide tents, prairie dogs, prairie fires, and many more things were different. The women had brought a small tent lodge with them. It was large enough for all four of them. The poles for the tent were used as a drag to carry their possessions with them. Inside the tent lodge, a small fire could be built that was not visible from outside the tent. The peak of the tent could be adjusted to use the breeze to draw the smoke out the top. Their knowledge of the prairie and the people that lived on it was very informative.

By midday they made it to the abandon Red Rock Village. They approached cautiously, watching for signs of the Redface. The village looked as they had abandoned it, except there were no bodies of Redface; instead, there were signs that a couple of large fires were built. In the fire ashes were fragments of burnt bone that looked like that of man. Little Rose explained to their companions what had happened here.

They camped near the narrows before the sight of the first battle in the valley. The two ladies from the prairie had many questions. They had seen the mountains from the prairie but did not know that people could live among the great centennials of their land. They thought that the mountains were the edge of the world. Snow managed to spear a few fish for dinner as Little Rose dug some roots to roast and eat.

Snow said, "I wonder if our people are spotting our fire. One small fire will not bring out the warriors. Maybe a scouting party."

The next day, they passed the place of the second battle of the River Village. The smell of the rotting bodies made all feel ill. After they were away from the smell, Little Rose explained to their two traveling companions what had happened. They both told Little Rose that they wanted to be just like her.

They were greeted as if they had been gone for a very long time. Yes, their fire was spotted. One small fire brought curiosity, though it was of no real concern. While they were gone, there had been more lodges built. The village seemed to be in harmony. The ex-slaves and Redface women appeared to be a part of the village. They were working hard to be part of the community. They appreciated their freedom and not getting beaten regularly. Some were taken as second wives by many men. The first wives accepted the situation, as long as they were not ignored by their husbands. Two wives divided up the work and helped in child upbringing. It was their law. For a man to accept a second wife, his first wife had to approve of his choice in front of the village people. It was a joining of three with the same ceremony. They had to all accept each other. The blood of all three had to flow together. The three bonding would rub their bleeding palms together, from one to the other, becoming as one.

Snow attended council. He told of their neighbors that were their cousins, of their victorious fight with the Redface, and of a good source of flint, showing what they had brought. He told of their neighbors need of salt which they had more than they needed. Snow agreed to show the traders the way. After a couple of days of rest, he would go with a party of traders, all carrying salt. All the men were impressed with the flint that Snow had brought back. Snow suggested that they made a small camp partway up the mountain on the other side of the river as a lookout. It had a good view of most of the valley, especially toward the Red Rock Village. It was closer than the present lookouts. Some had seen their fire after they left on their journey. It was decided two fires would be warning, and three fires was an emergency. An attack was imminent. Two bonded couples volunteered to establish the camp. Every five sleeps, they would be relieved.

The two ladies that had come with them spent the night in Snow's lodge. They were in awe of the bear hide that they slept on.

The next day, Snow and Little Rose went hunting. It had been several days since they were alone. They took the opportunity to be close, sharing in joining with each other. Again, Little Rose shot a nice deer. Snow was supposed to be the great hunter. His wife regularly showed him up. They got back to camp early enough to start making their guests their own bows. Little Rose and the two women started to be good friends. They worked well together, skinning the deer, then drying some of the deer's meat.

In private, Little Rose told Snow, "The two women had been hurt really bad by men when they were still girls. It continued until they were rescued. They do not want to be touched by any man. They believe that they had been torn up inside as girls, so they could not have babies. Although it had been several years where men had forced themselves on them most every night and also during the day, by many men, they had never gotten pregnant."

The next day was fishing. They also completed the two bows for their guests. Little Rose started to train the women, two more archers willing to protect their freedom.

Snow left early in the morning with five other men; two of which were regular traders. They all carried as much salt as they thought that they safely could. Little Rose would stay at home. Snow asked her nicely, telling her that he would only be a few days. The village needed her to train the archers and to train them in stealthily moving in the woods.

The report was that no new fires were spotted, and the camp at the other side of the lake only had a few small fires. They camped near what was the Red Rock Village. At sunset on the second day, they headed up the path to the Village of Falling Waters. They were met by a group of warriors halfway up. Snow was greeted as a returning hero. The village was keeping a lookout on duty at all times; they saw them coming. Their journey had been uneventful. After introductions, they unloaded their burden of salt. Snow was asked what they wanted in return.

Snow replied, "Some of your good gray flint."

The villagers thought they were getting a great trade, stone for salt.

The travelers were invited to council. Their hosts soon told Snow's traveling companions of how he had organized then led their people in a great victory over the Redface. Snow was a great warrior and a hero to all. Snow's traveling companion told of the great, enormous brown bear he had killed and how he had planned and led his people in three great victorious battles against the Redface. They embarrassed Snow. He did not want to hear any more "Uhs."

Snow told the council, "I am not a great warrior or hunter. I am just lucky." This just got him more praise with many more "Uhs."

They stayed one day, rested up, enjoying the hospitality. If nothing else, bringing salt made them honored guests. Snow asked of the women who were captured and rescued that chose to stay with them. He was informed that they were hardworking. It appeared that they would be an asset to their community. They would continue to watch them closely. They had caused no trouble. There was talk of some men taking second wives. There was a lot more women than men. Their lookouts had not spotted any fires approaching their village. That was good news.

That evening, they had a feast and fire in their honor. There were many demands for Snow to tell his story of killing the great bear. Snow relented, telling the story of how a bear killed himself on his spear as he was knocked unconscious by the bear.

In the morning, they loaded as much flint as they could safely carry. They were joined by two men from the Village of Falling Waters. They also carried a load of flint. They wanted to know the trail to the River Village. They were escorted to the prairie where they were given a sincere send-off.

On the second evening, they arrived in the River Village. Except for all being tired carrying their loads, the trip was uneventful. The flint was placed in the council lodge for future distribution to the many who would need some. Their guests were introduced. They were received with respect, being treated as long-lost cousins as they were. Snow was dragged off into the woods where he was mauled by his wife; she had missed him.

That evening they had a bonfire in honor of their guests. Snow and Little Rose demonstrated dancing together that they had learned in the Valley Village. Their two guests joined in teaching a couple of young ladies how. Soon, many were participating. It was a lot of fun. It was a relief from all the troubles.

In a couple of days, their guests left but not before telling many of how Snow was a great hero to their people. They each carried a load of salt with them. Snow and Little Rose escorted them to the abandoned Red Rock Village, half way home for them. Promises were made to continue to trade, and if necessary, they could join in the defense of their valleys. Snow and Little Rose spent the night a little way from the Red Rock Village. They were looking forward to not having to share their lodge. They made plans to help their guests build their own lodge.

When they returned the next day to their village, they were informed that the council had decided to attack the Redface camp on the other side of the Red Rock Lake. Snow was made the war chief for the attack. Snow went to council, warning of the hazards. Their minds were made up. They wanted Snow to plan, then lead the attack. Snow could not refuse, even though he thought that there were others who could do better.

Returning from the meeting Little Rose told Snow, "You are a respected leader. You give people confidence. Many will hesitate unless you lead." Snow thought even his wife will not give him any peace about being a hero.

The new lookout station seemed to be working out well, providing a good early warning to the village. Snow and Little Rose would scout ahead, leaving a day before their soldiers. Some of the soldiers would remain at the village for defense in case things went wrong. Snow and Little Rose would meet the others in the Red Rock Village. Their soldiers were well trained and in high spirits. Over half of their soldiers were women, some wanting revenge for their previous mistreatment or the loss of a loved one. Their warriors, spear-throwers, and archers were formed into groups. Each group had its own leader. They had three groups of eight warriors, ten archers, and six spear-throwers each. The warriors were also spear-throwers. They used heavier spears that could penetrate into a lodge and still kill. They were ready.

CHAPTER 6

Snow and Little Rose went to the abandon Red Rock Village where they hid most of their gear, wanting to travel light. At the break of daylight, they headed out over the prairie. They wanted to avoid the established trails next to the lake and river. The prairie was new to them. There were no trees to hide behind; the ground was flat. They soon realized that they had to travel crouched over to try to stay below the high grasses. The prairie was not as flat as it first appeared; there were small ridges and ravines. There were some dried-out creek beds that were good places to hide. By midday they were not as near to the camp as they wanted to be. Snow was to continue while Little Rose was to go back to hold the troops at the Red Rock Village until Snow had done his scouting. They should have planned an additional day. Snow took a short route near the river to where he was in sight of the camp. There were no guards to be seen. He was almost seen by two boys fishing. He had to remain hidden in the tall grass, he did not want to be detected. It was almost an hour while the boys argued over who had caught the biggest fish. Snow did not understand their language, though the argument was obvious. He eventually was able to get a good look of the camp. It appeared to be mainly women. There was several warriors seen. One man was viciously beating a woman, then he made her get on all fours, having his way with her. Everyone else in their camp seemed to ignore his attack. Snow had seen enough. He headed back. The moon was waning not yet up, once it arose it would be half full. It got very dark so Snow had to stop, waiting for the moon to rise. Eventually, he could see to travel the trail next to the lake. He made it back at daybreak. Little Rose first hugged him, happy to see him, then she got angry at him for he had scared her. Snow got a punch in his stomach.

Snow gave an order that all relax and rest up with no fires. A few warriors accompanied by a few archers were sent on the trail to the lake as guards, with the orders that if they were detected, they had to kill the offenders. Their presence must not be revealed. By midafternoon, they started down the trail, traveling till near dark. They dispersed at the far end of the lake, an hour's walk to the camp. There they waited until the first hint of daybreak. The Redface camp was set up next to the river. One of their groups followed Snow to the far side of the camp. In a half hour, Little Rose led her group to the center, away from the camp. The last group crept up the trail directly at the camp. They surrounded the enemy's camp. They positioned themselves, covering the entire area. A mourning dove hooted in an unusual tone, then a duck quacked in an odd sort of way. Snow motioned that his people advance on the camp, slow and quiet. When they got within range, all stood. The sun had already risen. There were several men moving around. One man was near the river, squatting, trying to relieve himself. There was the call of a raven. The man squatting was rudely interrupted with several arrows penetrating his hide. The camp seemed to awake slowly. The screams were probably thought to be of women being abused. It was a surreal scene; by the time the alarm was sounded, many Redface were dead or incapacitated. The men and older boys refused to surrender; they all struggled till death. The final count: twenty-three Redface were killed, five older Redface boys were dead, and no villagers were wounded or killed. Twenty-two slaves were freed, seventeen Redface women were captured, and twelve children were taken into custody.

The women and children were gathered together. The ex-Redface women explained the situation to the women survivors. As soon as the situation was known, four Redface women had their throats slit. The men were stripped, their eyes were gouged out, and their private were cut off. The privates and eyes were thrown into a fire, then their bodies thrown into the river. Most all the soldiers turned their back as the body mutilations went on. When a woman would desecrate her husband's body, it was not a good relationship.

Returning to the abandoned Red Rock Village, five buffalo forded the river, crossing their path. Snow and Little Rose quickly put six arrows into one of the beast's chest and neck, bringing him down. Little Rose immediately said that Snow had delivered the fatal shot, not giving Snow a chance to rebuke the claim. Quickly, the beast was skinned and the meat removed. Some of the women and children were weak from hunger. It was decided that a fire be built on-site; all would have a lunch of buffalo meat. Snow was served the buffalo's roasted heart. He shared with some of the other men. It took three days to return to the River Village. Most of the remaining women and children were weak from hunger. Now Snow's lodge would have a bear hide and a buffalo hide for Little Rose and him to lie together.

Returning to the village, Snow and Little Rose were pronounced great warriors and hunters, something they did not want. They were becoming legends while they were still young.

No Redface fires could be seen near the villages. The invading Redface's current threat had been eliminated. Peace and tranquility again returned to the valleys for the most part. The women who joined the people were accepted and integrated with little problems. Many were taken as wives; they were reproducing as was appropriate. There were changes in their culture; women outnumbered men. Women were now a respected part of society, taking a respected place in the society. The women established their own council, which caused a lot of political discourse. The debate often overflowed into the lodges; on occasions, nooky was denied, as well as meals were not prepared. It became difficult for a husband to get abusive with two wives, especially when the wives were trained and blooded in combat. Most men accepted the changes. It was easier to get along. If they did not start any unreasonable fights with their wives, they were well taken care of by two wives or one loyal wife that did not want to share their loyal husband.

Snow managed to not get involved with the politics. He kept his mouth shut and just listened. He followed his father's rules when dealing with his wife. Following those rules, when Snow was challenged, Little Rose defended him with resolve. Sometimes the smartest thing to do was nothing.

Snow and Little Rose helped their two guest women, who they had brought back with them from the battle of the Village of Falling Waters, build their own lodge. It became obvious that they did not want a man. They did not need a man. They had each other. They were discrete, not flaunting their choice of companions. This was accepted in the village. There was a lot of women to go around. They were helpful to their neighbors, always eager to help when work was to be done. They were well-liked and noncontroversial. They were an asset to the village. They both became excellent archers. They hunted together, often bringing fresh game to the village as well as helping gather grains and other foods.

Regular trade and communication were established with the neighboring valley. People started to reestablish the Red Rock Village and their fishing camp. A meeting was held of representatives of all five villages from both valleys at the Red Rock Village. Snow was appointed as a represented of the River Village. Many issues were discussed, from trade to mutual defense. Snow spent two days listening to many suggestions. Snow believed that his input was not needed. The other representatives were making a good agreement for all concerned. All agreed to a system of signaling of threats with fire signals.

The chief of the Valley Village, a representative, said, “Snow, we have not heard from you. I want your thoughts.”

Snow said, “I believe that the Redface will return. Maybe not in our lifetime, maybe tomorrow. There might be other threats that we will face. If we can talk and agree, when a threat comes, we will be stronger standing together. This agreement makes us stronger.” Snow got many “Uhs” in agreement. Rumors were spread that Snow said it was a good agreement, so it had to be good. Again, Snow was getting credit.

The sun got lower in the sky. The mornings became chilly. The leaves changed color and were falling on the ground. Before heavy snow settled in, Snow and Little Rose spent three days climbing to the pass to look out over the prairie. There were several fires in the foothills between the mountains and the prairie. It looked to be several small camps. Farther out on the prairie along the great river, there were several fires to be seen. These were what they had seen on their previous climbs. There were no fires that gave them concerns, although there was curiosity about the fires in the foothills. They had brought a small shelter tent made from hides and a fur blanket. They cuddled close against the cold. When they awoke, there was several inches of new snow. Little Rose took one more look down toward the foothills. She saw something moving below in the snow. Initially, they believed that it was a bear. Looking closer, it was three objects, all about the same size. Bears did not travel in groups unless it would be a sow with cubs. The three objects were the same size, not a sow with cubs. Whatever it was, they were moving uphill toward them. Little Rose wanted to wait and see what it was. She believed they might be people. Snow did not argue with his wife; besides, they had their bows, and Snow a bear spear. They had the high ground; they were safe, except for a possible bear.

It was getting midday. Snow did not want to spend another night on the mountain. The three were definitely people. It looked like they were struggling; they were being followed by six other people. Little Rose was adamant that they stay and watch. Snow protested to no avail. He would not leave without Little Rose, even when she told Snow to leave.

By midafternoon, it appeared that pursuers were gaining on the pursued. Little Rose was convinced that it was three women pursued by six men. Snow told her that she had a vivid imagination. That was a mistake on Snow's part; now it was a matter of Little Rose proving herself right, a challenge.

It was a couple hours till sunset. The people had made progress coming up the mountain. It looked like Little Rose was right. It looked like it would not be long before the three women would be overtaken. Without warning, Little Rose headed down the mountain, saying, "I will try to save them."

Snow did not have a choice; he followed his wife. Little Rose was moving down the slope much too fast for safety. If she lost her footing, she would be tumbling uncontrolled down the mountain.

Snow struggled to keep up. Just as the three women were being surrounded, Little Rose was standing next to them, shooting arrows into the pursuers. Snow joined in. In short order, one man was left escaping down the mountainside. With two arrows in his back, he was tumbling down the mountain. He seemed to gain speed as he descended. The three women were holding up their hands, begging for mercy. The language and clothing made it clear that they were Redface. Why were three Redface women being pursued up a mountain by six Redface warriors? It was getting dark, with a cold wind blowing. A niche was found between several rocks. The five of them huddled together between the rocks. The three women were spent, welcoming any protection from their enemy as well as the cold.

As day broke, the wind stopped blowing; the five started up the slope. There were few words spoken between the three women. For Snow and Little Rose, a lot of their communication was not in words; words were not needed. It was late morning when they reached the top of the pass. Snow and Little Rose had left all their supplies on the top when they descended in a rush. Now they shared the dried meat, fruit, and berries that they had brought. It was obvious the three women did something that irked their taskmasters; they were avoiding possible death. They headed down the mountain. In two days, they were camped at the tree line. Two rabbits, a spruce hen, and wood to make a fire was welcome. The three Redface women seemed to be quiet and submissive to follow along, accepting their fate with Snow and Little Rose. The three women cleaned and cooked the game as well as eating their share. Tomorrow they should be home.

After returning, the story of the three women was told. One of them had been released after being captured near the Village of Falling Waters at the Redface camp battle.

One of the women was being held down because she had displeased a Redface chief; the chief was prepared to gouge her eyes out. The other two women, including the one that had been previously captured, were watching; one grabbed a spear and the other, a knife. The chief had the spear thrust into his throat. The Redface warrior that was holding down the woman had a knife thrust into the base of his skull. All three women knew that their lives would end in misery.

They knew that the village people lived over the mountain, their only chance for survival. They begged for mercy, agreeing to be mindful slaves. They were granted freedom and given the opportunity to join the River Village, which they gratefully accepted and promised that they would defend the village with their lives.

Little Rose told Snow, "I told you that word would spread where the Redface would feel the ire of their women."

Snow replied, "You were right. Two Redface warriors died."

Little Rose said, "Eight Redface warriors. Every woman in that Redface camp knows what happened. They know that the six warriors were sent to kill the women did not return. The story will spread. Every Redface women and the Redface slaves will hear the story. Eventually, the story will be that it was many women killed many Redface warriors. More stories will spread. The Redface women and the slaves will be embraved. Soon the Redface warriors will be sleeping with one eye open."

The days became short, and the snow got deep. Snow and Little Rose did all their hunting near the village on snowshoes. Little Rose killed her first elk; it was a large bull. It took several people two days to bring all the meat to the village. The fresh meat was shared and appreciated by all. The heavy snow brought the elk into the bottom of the valley. Several hunters got elk and deer. It was a good winter for the village. There had been many births and few deaths. As the snow melted, the river overflowed its banks. The river had many fish on their spring run. The fish were easy to catch as they tried to lay their eggs in the still water. The village celebrated the spring with a feast of delicious roe. The traders left for their first trip of the year to the Village of Falling Waters with their load of salt. The traders would also take the news and bring back flint and the news of the other villages.

Lookouts would be sent to look for fires from several lookout camps located in varied observation spots. News came from the Lake Village and Red Rock Village. All had had a good winter. Now they waited to hear from the Valley Village and the Village of Falling Waters. When the snow cleared enough, Snow and Little Rose would climb the mountain to check on the other side. The three women who had been rescued just before winter became a part of the village, providing additional information on the Redface. There were several uprisings with their women. The Redface solution was to kill all women who rebelled. The conclusion was that the Redface would have a shortage of women to serve them; more would have to captured. The rescued women said that a lot of the pregnant Redface women were sticking sticks up in themselves until it hurt then walking around with the sticks in them, killing their babies while they were very tiny. They did not want to bring children into the Redface world. Word was spreading among women in the Redface camps that there were other ways to live.

The news came that in the villages in the other valley had a good winter. Several fires were spotted on the prairie; every few days, they were moving closer to the valleys. Snow was again made a member of the war council; he was to lead the archers.

Snow and Little Rose went for a long walk to talk; some of their talk was of family and friends, neither wanted to confront the news of the Redface nearing their valley.

Little Rose finally spoke of what was bothering both of them. "We must get our people ready to fight."

Snow responded, "I do not want another summer of war. I do not want to be responsible for more deaths."

"If you want, I will run away with you."

"I am ready to go. When do we leave?"

Little Rose answered, "Let us leave as soon as the Redface treat is no more."

Snow agreed, "I agree with you."

The snow was still deep; it took four days to get to the top of the pass. The only fire that they could see that was of concern was on the other side of the Red Rock Lake, two or three days' walk from the lake. In three more days, Snow and Little Rose were talking to the Redface woman they rescued last fall. All three had taken up archery and were part of Little Rose's team. The council was pushing Snow to make a plan to attack the Redface. Snow realized that in the previous battles, they had surprise and luck on their side. He could not count on that continuing. Snow concluded it was like facing a bear.

He wanted to turn and run; to turn and run meant death, exposing your back.

Spotting indicated it appeared there was one large Redface camp. I was near the far side of the Red Rock Lake.

Snow needed to know how many Redface warriors there were, if they had adopted other weapons, and what were their plans. He got two volunteers: Big Smile, the Redface woman who was rescued in the fall and the woman who had been sent on her way at the Village of Falling Water by the Redface camp; and Three Doves, the woman who Big Smile saved that was going to get her eyes gouged out. They would go into the Redface camp and spy on them. They said that men were careful. If they used or beat another man's woman without his permission, he had a right to kill the offending man. In the winter, the big camps were broken into many small camps. In spring, camps would join together; often they would be groups from other areas that would join in the larger camps. Everybody did not know each other. If they went into the village, pretending to be the women of a man from another area, they would not be questioned, especially if they looked to belong to a strong man. A plan was made; Snow did not totally trust the women, so he did not tell them all his plan.

Snow, Little Rose, Big Smile, Three Doves, two archers, and two warriors left the River Village for the Red Rock Village. Not revealed to the Redface women, the next days they would be followed by forty archers, twenty-five warriors, and ten spear-throwers as part of the attacking army if the war council called for an attack. Snow had to know what he was against before he could make a detailed plan.

When they reached the Red Rock Village, Big Smile and Three Doves put on old clothes that were tattered and dirty. To Snow and Little Rose's horror, Big Smile took a knife, cutting her head letting the blood flow into her hair. Big Smile then took a stick then proceeded to beat Three Doves until her ear and jaw were bleeding; she was also struck on the nose, which would blacken her eyes. Three Doves then took the stick beating Big Smile. They explained that if they looked abused, they would be less suspect. Such a beating would speak well of their man, a man who enjoyed giving pain; it would say they had a strong man. Big Smile and Three Doves walked into the prairie. They said that they did not wanted to look as if they were coming down a path without a man. They would sneak into the camp. Nobody would pay much attention to two beaten women if they acted meek and submissive doing their man's work.

The new Red Rock Village was reestablished a little upriver from the original site. It was placed so it could be defended easier; on one side was the river and on the other the Red Rock Cliff. The arriving force went to work. They placed lines of sharpened stakes in front of the village, trying to make them hidden in leaves. If stepped on, they would be painful. Positions were made for the archers and spear-throwers with sharpened stakes in front of their positions. They tried to make their position look weaker than it would be, hoping to get the Redface to attack in force. Some of the warriors would be concealed on the flanks with throwing spears. Once the Redface attacked and were engaged, the archers would appear from their hidden positions, then the warriors would close around the attackers, cutting off their retreat. The whole plan depended on the number of Redface. If there were too many Redface, the plan could be modified to not decimate them but repel them. Within the next two days, they were expecting reinforcements from the neighboring valley's villages and the Lake Village. Their army would be over a hundred fighters; over half would be women. A year previous, this kind of force was not imaginable by any of the defenders. Guards were posted, lookouts were observing. There were reports of fires that indicated a large camp; smoke plumes could be seen during the day.

It was late morning, the reinforcements were expected at any time; yells and screams were heard from the path to the lake. Snow, Little Rose, and several of the archers and warriors went to investigate. On the path, between the cottonwood trees, came Three Doves running, followed by many women; they were followed by Redface warriors throwing spears and swinging their war axes at the stragglers. Little Rose drew her bow and placed an arrow into the neck of one of the Redface that was prepared to dispatch a woman with his war ax. The other archers followed suit. The village warriors launched their throwing spears. As more Redface poured onto the scene, they were joined by more village archers and warriors. Many of the women coming from the Redface camp picked up weapons and lined up with the village people, joining the fight. More village fighters came and joined the battle as more Redface came down the path. The village archers were taking a toll on the advancing Redface, but the Redface throwing spears were deadly when they made their mark. Snow stopped one of the Redface spears with his leg; he continued to fight. It started to look as if the villagers were going to be overran when the reinforcements from the Valley Villages showed up, running across the open ground, joining the battle. More people were lying on the ground, wounded or dead, than were standing; still, the battle continued. The archers and spear-throwers were out of projectiles on both sides. War axes were being swung with an occasional picked up spear used as a hand spear. The village soldiers were being forced into a circle, fighting back-to-back, when the reinforcements arrived from the Lake Village, joining the battle. Neither side seemed to have an obvious advantage when Big Smile came down the path with many women swinging war axes. The tide of the battle turned; the exhausted Redface quickly fell to the hatred of their women. Dead bodies and wounded fighters were strewn about; some were lying on top of each other. They were intermixed; Redface and villagers were on top and next to each other in no pattern. Little Rose's left forearm was broken, it happened as she fended off a blow from a war ax; the handle hit her arm, not the ax head. She continues swinging her war ax with her right hand. Snow was weak; he had lost a lot of blood. Those still standing started to aid the wounded. The women from the Redface camp, many being slaves, quickly dispatched the surviving Redface warriors.

It was several days before relief arrived from the villages. Thirty-seven villager men and fifty-one village women died. Fifty-two Redface women and slaves died; some were killed by their own slaves, but most died helping the villagers. The Redface toll of men killed was hard to determine. A few had been killed in their camp. Their bodies were mutilated, many of the bodies were thrown into the river and lake. Most agreed that over ninety Redface warriors were killed. Both Big Smile and Three Doves were killed fighting for their freedom. Snow was the only member of the war council to survive. He could only stand on one leg using a stick for a crutch; Soaring Raven, Snow's father, was among the dead. Four of the five village chiefs were also killed. Seventeen Redface women and slaves wanted to stay with the villagers, becoming free. The death of so many chiefs and elders was a great loss. Over half of the village people that went to war had perished. Some were young, not yet adults.

No one seemed to know what Big Smile and Three Doves did in the Redface camp. Some of the surviving women said that they convinced the women to rebel against their oppressors. Others said they killed a couple men who were beating a woman. One report said they killed the Redface chief and his wife, a cruel woman.

It was another eight sleeps before Snow and Little Rose hobbled into the River Village. They were concerned that they would not be welcome; they felt responsible for so many losses. Would they be blamed for the loss of so many loved ones?

Snow told Little Rose, "That is the third time I lived when I should have died."

They were treated as heroes; they were offered food and drink. They stopped at Snow's father's lodge. Snow's mother, Spring Flower; Snow; Little Rose; and Snow's two sisters wrapped their arms around each other, grieved for their loss.

The lookouts reported that there was nothing of concern. Snow thought to himself that the immediate threat was gone. So many dead for what? His ancestors faced a similar problem; they ran away, finding peace for ten generations. Maybe that was the best solution; the world looked to be big.

It was hard to walk through the village. Most every lodge had lost at least one family member—a father, mother, son, or daughter; some lodges had multiple losses. One lodge was empty—both mother and father were lost. Now their three children lived in an uncle's lodge. Their aunt was also lost. The man was now taking care of six children, three of his own and three of his brother's. Snow saw White Dove staring at him with hate in her eyes. He had jilted her, the prettiest girl in the village, for a skinny little runt. He was responsible that so many women were brought into the village that she could not even be a second wife and slept alone. Now her father, older brother, and sister were dead; it was all Snow's fault. Little Rose also grieved. She had lost her sister and her older brother. She was the woman who trained women to use bows. So many women had died; maybe women should not be soldiers. Snow and Little Rose agreed there were no victors in war; it was who lost the least.

CHAPTER 7

Snow and Little Rose had to get away. They could go and look for a peaceful valley, fulfilling their promise to each other. Snow's leg was working well enough that he could walk a reasonable day's walk, but his running was not good. Little Rose's arm was healing, wrapped in heavy elk hide. She was warned to not pull a bow or lift anything with it. Her arm would still break easily. It would be midsummer before she was back to normal.

They went by the way of the Red Rock Village. They were welcome in the village as returning heroes. That gave them a morale boost until they passed the battle site with numerous piles of rocks; most were decorated with bright-colored hide, feathers, and a few personal items of the fallen.

After another day's walk, they were at the Village of Falling Waters; another hero's welcome. Snow and Little Rose agreed it was hard to be heroes when one was surrounded by ghosts.

They headed up the mountain to the north. They hiked till they reached the tree line. Snow shot a rabbit. The berries were thick. They ate well. Sleep had become hard for both of them; they would be awakened by bad dreams. If it had not been for each other's support, they would have become like the crazy old woman. They headed east toward the rising sun, often climbing higher to get snow for water, then sitting together holding hands and admiring their world. As the days went by, the thin, fresh air seemed to rinse out some of the bloodstains that saturated their memories.

After days, they did not count they had gone as far east as they could. The entire morning was in the shadow of an enormous mountain. Along the way, they had seen elk, deer, and magnificent bighorn sheep; they had no desire to shoot one but instead felt comforted watching them. They seemed to be getting used to the thin air. The flow of life seemed steady, going in a smooth rhythm.

They headed south toward a pass. They wondered what was on the other side. This was big country; it took three days to reach the pass. There was a well-used game trail up through the pass. Far in the distance, they could see several white-topped mountains. They camped for the night, sleeping under the stars. They discussed how high they would have to climb to touch the heavens. Maybe the air would get so thin that they could not breathe. Only the great spirits could touch the stars.

When morning came, they proceeded south; finally, they reached the south edge of the pass, looking down upon a huge valley. The valley floor was covered with a thick forest; they could see glimpses of a river, snaking itself through the valley. The valley and river flowed toward the setting sun, west. They could see many elk on the mountainside grazing.

Their worst fear, a large brown bear, was coming up from the valley below, right toward them. Snow quickly looked around, picked a spot. He told Little Rose to get behind him; he prepared with his spear as Little Rose prepared with a throwing spear. It was an enormous bear. It was eating berries as it went. The bear meandered around them to a bright spot of blue and red berries, filled its mouth, then walked past them, down the other side of the pass. Had the bear not seen them, or was he satisfied with berries to eat? The bear had not tasted the air as Snow knew that bears did. Snow and Little Rose sat on a rock, holding hands, looking down at the valley, they discussed why the bear had not eaten them.

Snow commented, "We have not had a bath in a long time. Maybe he did not like our smell."

Little Rose agreed, "You cannot go any lower than when a bear does not want to eat you."

Snow said, "Let us go down to that river and have a bath."

It took two days to get to the river; there was no sign of man. The woods were abundant in flora and fauna. The river ran wide, deep, and sweet, with an abundance of fish, beaver, otter, and other life. A good bath, nice fire, fish for supper, along with some good roots roasted; life was good. They started to walk downstream along the river; the valley was large and filled with everything a man needed. There were several small lakes along the way. After several days, the valley looked to come to an end ahead; it looked like the river flowed into a wall of rock.

After another day's walk, they could not see how to continue; the river flowed in a torrent through a wide crack in the mountain ahead. They had not seen any sign of man in the valley, not even a small fire in the dark when they went up the valley sides for a look. They had a large productive valley all to themselves. The game did not seem to be afraid of them. It was hard to understand that they were able to walk up close to deer, then the deer would move out of the way.

They started to look around. Was there another way out of this valley, or would they have to go back the way they came? All the mountains around them seemed too high to climb, except the way they came in. They examined the river exit. There was no way through the torrent of water. The sound of the water through the rock walls sounding like a large animal growling in deafening defiance.

They started to walk along the rock wall to the north. There was another crack in the mountain; dirt and debris had worked itself into the crack, leaving a depression next to the mountain. Investigating the crack, they could not be seen through. There was a trail going into the crack that looked like many animals were using the crack. It was wide enough that two people could walk side by side. Snow with Little Rose, following carefully entered; their curiosity was leading them into the unknown. The path headed downward in a moderate slope, first curving to the right then to the left. After what seemed to be a long way, Snow stopped; Little Rose moved up beside him. They instinctively held hands as they looked out over the prairie.

Although they had only been bonded in marriage for two years, their bond went back to a pesky little girl wanting to aggravate a quiet, shy boy. The last two years of turmoil standing together had strengthened their bond. In most things, they were as one. They shared joy and grief.

Snow said, “The path made by animals says that it goes through.”

Little Rose said, “Where on the prairie will it come out? Can we find our way home across the prairie, or do we have to go back?”

“Only one way to find out.”

The crack opened out onto a cliff facing the prairie.

Snow said, “Look, I think that this is the start of the great river that runs across the prairie. We must be on the lookout for Redface. Their fires say that they like to camp next to the great river.”

Nature had piled rocks up against the cliff. To the right, there was a narrow path downward. The path curved to the left onto a mound, then continued curving all the way around where it came near where the river came out of the mountain. Here, the water rushed out of the mountain onto a large pile of rocks, making many small pools of water. Then the water cascaded into a series of large pools. Here, the roar of the water echoing out of the crack was deafening.

Little Rose commented, “It is like the mouth of a giant bear.”

Snow agreed, “Yes, the bears mouth.”

It was getting late. They decided to return up the path to the valley to spend the night where they felt safe from the Redface. The moon was waxing; it would set after the sun, casting its light after sunset. After sunset, they went through the crack to stand at the cliff, looking for fires on the prairie. They saw fires. They looked to be along the river, at a distance that would not be of any immediate threat. They sat on a small ledge, talking as they enjoyed the moonlight view.

Snow said, “We found our peaceful valley.”

“Yes, it will be a wonderful home for many.”

“It is big enough for all our people to live in peace and prosperity. It is secluded, hard to find, and will be easy to defend.”

Little Rose asked, “Do we bring our people here?”

Snow answered, “Do we? Will they want to come? The decision is not up to us.”

It looked like the mountain that they came out of was the farther toward the setting sun, west. They knew that they had gone west in the valley. They could go toward the Big Dipper, north, along the mountains; that should bring them home. In the morning, they departed, passing near the Bear's Mouth then walking north. After a day's walk, they were still next to the mountain; they saw no more cracks or water flows. They were following a path that looked to be made by animals. The mountain was almost a sheer cliff; there was no place to climb up except the loose rocks next to the edge. They had managed to take what was known as a prairie chicken. They camped, foraging enough wood for a small cooking fire. The prairie chicken was larger than their spruce hen. The meat seemed juicer. It was quite good. They set up their small tent next to the sheer mountain wall. They slept well.

Toward the end of the next day, they heard what sounded like the Bear's Mouth. They came to a small river coming out of a wide crack in the mountain wall. There was a huge rock in the center dividing the stream into two. One side had a heavy flow of water where the other side had only a small flow. Their curiosity was irresistible. They left their camp gear. It was a steep and slippery climb into the side with only a trickle of water, not a short way. They came out in a valley that looked like the valley that was home to the Village of Falling Waters and Valley Village. Again, it was decision time: spend the night; explore this valley, leaving their gear on the other side of the wall; leave it unexplored; or go out, camp for the night, and come back tomorrow. There was no sign of people. They would spend the night. The weather looked good. There was an overhang on the wall near the river. They would sleep there. It did not take Snow long to make a fishing spear and get a couple of nice fish while Little Rose made a fire. Little Rose also found a couple of roots to roast. They had a delicious dinner. In the middle of the night, it started to rain heavily. The overhang kept them dry.

When they woke in the morning, they realized they had a problem. The rain had swollen the river; now the second stream had a good flow of water. Snow and Little Rose decided to take the opportunity to explore. Surveying the mountains, they could not see a pass that might be used to climb out of the valley. They were surrounded by high mountains. They walked upstream. It was not long until they saw deer, rabbit, spruce hen, otter, muskrat, and a variety of other animals. Roots, berries, and a variety of other edible plants and herbs were abundant. In the river gravel, they found heavy yellow soft stones; they could be easily pounded into different shapes. These were rare; they were prized for ornaments. They each picked up a handful to take home for gifts. They spent the next two days exploring the valley. It had everything needed for a medium-sized village to prosper. The river had gone down a little. They snared a rabbit and gathered a few more roots; again they had a delicious dinner. They named the valley Little Bear Valley. The other valley would be Big Bear Valley for their loudmouths.

In the morning, they decided to try to get out; the water had gone down a little more. Snow went first. After two steps, his feet were washed out from under him. He came out the bottom traveling fast, flying butt-first into the pond below.

Little Rose's voice could be heard, sounding like she was hollering into a hollow log. "Are you all righty? Talk to me. Please talk to me."

Snow answered, "I am all right. It is easy. You can just slide down. Sit in the center and let go."

Little Rose asked, "Are you sure?"

Snow replied, "I am sure. Trust me."

As Little Rose sat down, she said, "I trust you."

Little Rose came out screaming; skipped once on her butt across the water. Snow was laughing when Little Rose came out of the water. Snow got a punch in the stomach.

Snow said, "It is like being tickled with a blade of grass. I thought it was fun."

Little Rose said, "You should have warned me. No nooky for you."

They got their gear that had not been disturbed; continuing on their way. By midday they were laughing about their ride on the water. They both agreed. If they could get up the stream easier, they would go again. Snow started thinking. How could one get up to the valley when the water was high. Maybe use a log like they use to cross a river.

Snow and Little Rose saw vultures and eagles circling a short distance from the mountain. They dropped their gear, moving quietly through the trees and thick tall grass. Soon they came across a small party of about eight men skinning two buffalo. They did not look like Redface. Their clothing and weapons were wrong.

To Snow's surprise, Little Rose stood up, calling, "We are friends. We are travelers."

She did not only surprise Snow; she surprised the men skinning the buffalo.

The men stood, looking at her, as Little Rose repeated, "Friend." She smiled and waved with open hands.

Snow stood slowly, not wanting to do anything that might look aggressive.

As the men looked on, Little Rose walked toward them, again saying, "Friend."

Snow followed slowly, wondering what his wife got him into. After the initial scare, the men seemed to be more curious. Who was this woman?

After a little awkwardness, it was apparent that these men were not Redface. Their language was similar to theirs. They were plains people who were also enemies of the Redface. They were great in numbers. They told of attacking a large Redface camp and killing many. They told of the summer before last when they had a great war with the Redface. They told of how their leaders met with the Redface leaders, telling the Redface, "Attack us and we will kill you, giving your women freedom. Touch one of our women, and we will cut the private off ten times ten Redface men."

Little Rose told how the village women left the dead Redface warriors. They also told the plains people of last summer and this spring of how the village people were attacked by Redface. Snow and Little Rose spent five days with the plains people. The plains people were experts with the throwing spear. Their archery techniques were not to the level of the village people. They exchanged stories and culture. They also gave each other training and tips in the use of weapons and tactics of war. Little Rose was again pulling her bow. Her arm had healed quickly. The plains women used smaller throwing spears than their men. Many wanted to become an archer when they saw Little Rose's abilities. The plains people marked their territory with a buffalo skull painted red; this was a warning to the Redface. Snow counseled with them, agreeing that he would tell his people of the plains people and how they were friends to be welcomed. Snow also told that he thought that a few of the rescued slaves in the villages were plains women. He would return them if they wanted to come. He could not force them because they were free by the village law. Snow explained to them where their valley was. Snow was hesitant of telling them of the valleys they had found. Snow tried to explain how they got here, crossing the mountains. They thought that the mountains were the end of the world. They did not understand going over them. Snow was told that the Big Bear Gods lived in the mountains and of how they ate people. Snow did not tell of his bear. They traded a couple of their heavy yellow soft stones for two buffalo skulls painted red that they could use to warn the Redface, letting the Redface know that the valley people were friends of the prairie people. The skulls would also tell the prairie people they would be welcome.

It was six sleeps' walk to the Village of Falling Waters. Snow and Little Rose were greeted with enthusiasm; the villagers had watched them leave on their trek. Many believed that they would never return. Snow counseled with the village men, telling them of the discovered valleys, their encounter with the prairie people, and how the prairie people could be considered friends. Snow presented them with a buffalo skull painted red. He explained the significance, telling them to place it where it would be seen at their valley's entrance. He told them it welcomed the plains people as welcomed guests, and they should be treated as cousins. The red buffalo skull was also a warning to the Redface, telling them that they were friends of the fearless plains people. The next morning, Snow and Little Rose went to the Valley Village; again Snow held council with the men, telling them what he had told the Village of Falling Waters men. Snow also told them of the red buffalo skull, its meaning, and they would see it where they left or entered their valley.

After two more sleeps, they arrived at the Red Rock Village. Again, a great welcome. Snow counseled with the men, presenting them with their red buffalo skull. Snow was informed that they had not seen any more sign of the Redface. Again, there was peace in the valley.

Another day and they were home. It became a celebration. The returning heroes and great adventurers returning home. Neither Snow nor Little Rose enjoyed their celebrity status; they would sooner be fishing, hunting, or just watching the water flow on its journey as they held hands. They did get pleasure working with people; showing them what they had learned. Little Rose was known as the greatest archer. All, especially the young women and girls, wanted to learn from her. The men wanted to practice with Snow with throwing spears.

Snow used two rocks, pounding a few of the heavy yellow soft stones out so he could punch a hole in each then attach each to its own leather thong. He and Little Rose gave them as gifts to their mothers and sisters to be worn about their necks. Little Rose also wore one.

CHAPTER 8

The days became short, the nights longer, and the leaves turned color, falling from the trees. Even though many had died in the war, many new people inhabited the villages. Many children were born, and many women were pregnant. It was getting harder to find game and edible roots, and herbs were getting scarce. The elk herd that was important to feed the village in the winter was getting smaller. The shaman warned of a hard winter.

The snow came early. It did not stop. Accumulating the snow made it very difficult to move about. The two women who had been badly abused by the Redface had taken in several orphan children, becoming a family.

It was a hard winter. The snow got deep. The wind blew cold and hard. People were still preparing for winter when the snows started. Food and firewood got scarce. Many shared lodgings; huddled together sharing their meager fire wood and food. The crazy woman moved in with the two women and their adopted children, sharing what they had. The crazy woman had hoarded some food, which she shared. The children started calling her grandmother.

Snow and Little Rose had also been warned by the crazy old woman that it would be a bad winter. Snow and Little Rose heeded her and the shaman's warnings and dried a lot of meat and fish; they had gathered a large pile of firewood. They had managed to down a large bull elk, which they cut into pieces. With a lot of difficulty through the deep snow, they managed to bring it to the village where they shared. During the worst of the winter weather, the midwife, now a widow, and her apprentice moved in with Snow and Little Rose.

Snow and Little Rose got little privacy. Often, they were kept up at night with the commotion of a birth. Little Rose helped with the births where she could. She got to hold the infants while they were cleaned up. Little Rose observed and listened closely. She felt that in an emergency, she could act as a midwife for a normal birth. For one difficult birth, the midwife cut the women open larger and reached into the woman, turning the baby around headfirst. The midwife took a porcupine sewing needle and sewed up the woman where she had cut her. The mother and baby thrived after a long healing process.

Spring came right on time. Warm with a bright sun melted the snow fast; the river flowed in a torrent. Some of the lodges that were near the river were washed away by the flooding. The early spring fish spawn did not yield many fish; the extremely high water made it difficult to catch fish. Edible roots and herbs were getting hard to find; when they would be found, they were small. Hunters had to go farther to get game. The second fish spawn was rewarding. Everyone had full bellies. Many fish were dried and stored away. The lodges that were lost were replaced with lodges farther from the river. The Redface women were helpful; with their use of hides, the new lodges had double walls. The Redface women shared their knowledge on how to store dried meat and fish in the space in the top of the lodge. A couple women from the prairie people showed how to smoke meat and preserve fish in salt. A larger area was cleared for the grain that was saved for seed; it was sowed. The hard winter and hunger had convinced all that food storage must be a priority.

The traders brought gray flint from the neighboring valley. They also brought word of a meeting at the next full moon at the Village of Falling Waters. All five villages were invited, as well as men from the prairie people were to come. Snow gave the traders a couple yellow soft stones for a load of flint. They said that four of the villages had survived the hard winter. They were on their way to the last village, the Lake Village. They would return in several days with news of the Lake Village.

The new chief, Bugling Elk, Two Otter, and Snow would go to the meeting representing the River Village.

In five days, the traders returned with three members of the Lake Village council. The Lake Village had survived the winter in good health. They were able to spear large fish in the lake all winter. Every winter they built lodges on the lake ice. Then they cut holes in the ice, where they speared fish through the holes.

In the morning the three traders and the six village representatives headed for the Red Rock Village; all carried a load of salt for their neighbors. It was not far until Snow heard a distinct cricket chirp. It would not feel normal for Snow without his shadow. How she moved through the woods so quietly was still a mystery to Snow.

The representatives and traders were welcomed by the Red Rock Villagers. They counseled together. A group of the plains people had a winter camp near the lake out in the prairie; the Fish Camp had been reestablished. Trade of fish and buffalo meat had helped both peoples have a good winter. The Red Rock Village and a tribe of plains people had formed a close relationship. Numerous buffalo skulls painted red could be seen on every path. Snow was shown their preparedness. All trained with weapons, including women and children. The plains people had great skills on the prairie. They sent out regular scouting missions looking for the Redface and buffalo. Red Rock warriors went with the prairie people where they were training in their ways. Snow knew that one of the reasons that his people had won two victories over the Redface in the valley was the fact that the Redface did know the woods. The Red Rock Villagers had hidden positions for their archers and spear-throwers on every approach.

The following evening, the group was greeted at the Village of Falling Waters. Representatives from five villages and four tribes of prairie people were to counsel the next day.

Bugling Elk said, "Snow, you will speak for our village."

Snow asked, "Why do you chose me? You are our chief."

Bugling Elk replied, "I am a chief of one village. You are known by many."

Snow asked, "What am I going to say?"

Bugling Elk answered, "You will know what to say."

Twenty-seven men from five villages and four plains people tribes counseled together. Never before had there been such a council. The reason they gathered together was a common threat, the Redface. All agreed that they were stronger together. Each got an opportunity to say their peace. Some wanted to make a large war party and find and kill all the Redface. Others wanted to try to lure the Redface into a trap. There was a report from one of the prairie tribes that they had Redface women and escaped slave women showing up at their camp asking for help. The women said they had killed several Redface warriors then escaped while most of their warriors were out on a raid. The tribal representative said that they took the women in; they worked hard and caused no trouble. Snow told of the three women they aided in escaping their Redface masters. There was a lot of talk that the Redface women and slaves would be the Redface's demise. After a long day, all the representatives agreed to a stand together to defend all from the Redface. They also made plans to communicate among each other. All would continue monitoring the Redface's movements. All also agreed to free Redface slaves when they could. Some believed that the Redface would bring about their own demise with their cruelty to women.

Snow announced, "My wife and I found a beautiful valley to the south. We plan to establish a village there. All that wanted to live in peace in a peaceful valley are welcome to join us. Now there are no people living there. It would be easy to defend. Those interested can see me or Little Rose. We plan to remain committed to our neighbors in the defense against the Redface."

Many wanted to know how to get to his valley. Snow explained the little bear's mouth then the big bear's mouth. A few of the plains people had been to the big bear's mouth but did not know of a way through the mountain. To them the mountains were the edge of the world with a few valleys into the mountains where some people lived.

Returning to the Valley Village, Snow and Little Rose were asked by many about the new valley. Many wanted to go with them to settle a new valley. The moon started to wane. They planned to move to Big Bear Valley as the moon was half full, waxing. That gave them fifteen sleeps to prepare. It was spring, a time when all felt greatly refreshed. The fish spawns brought an abundance. Many berries were ripening. The rains brought green to the valley. The elk and deer were producing the next generation as most all the animals were. It was a time of hard work and many rewards.

It was also a time that brought sorrow. Snow's mother was having headaches, then she died in her sleep. Snow grieved for three days. He set at a secluded spot next to the river watching the water flow on its way.

Little Rose came sitting next to Snow, telling him, "I need you. Your two sisters need you. Your people need you. How long are you going to grieve?"

"I should have died at least three times, yet here I am. I am tired. I do not know if I have anything left in me to give. I have become many things I do not want to be."

"People look up to you. You set an example that all admire. People will follow you. You are a great leader and hero."

"I never wanted to be a great hunter, warrior, leader, or an example for others. I long for the simple pleasures."

"I also long for the simple pleasures. I want to feel my husband's love and passion. I want to give my husband my love and passion."

Little Rose gave herself, and Snow gave back.

The trek started. Snow led. Little Rose and some of her archers would bring up the rear. It was mainly the younger people. Included was the midwife's apprentice and her husband, now a full-fledged midwife with her own apprentice, one of Snow's sisters. The shaman's daughter, who had learned from her father and who had lost her husband in the war, would be their shaman. The two women who did not want men, along with their seven adopted children, came. The crazy woman, now called grandma by all, was coming. Little Rose's mother and brother were coming along. A few people from the Lake Village joined, including Setting Owl, his wife, and children. Setting Owl was known to make things. Several freed slaves and Redface women were eager to see this new valley; a new start in a new homeland. Several adolescent girls were following Little Rose, and several adolescent boys wanted to follow Snow. Many young that had lost their families in the war were going to a new home. Some people wanted to leave their families to be a part of a new future that they could help create.

As they passed the Red Rock Village, others joined. More joined as they passed the Village of Falling Waters. A few prairie people joined in. In all, there were sixty-three souls: seventeen men, twenty-one women, and twenty-five children. Many had drags transporting their possessions, food, clothing, many tent shelters, tools, and other needed goods; some drags were pulled by two children. Snow was pulling a drag with their bear and buffalo hide, along with a hide tent shelter and several fur blankets along with several tools.

The progress was slow with their heavy loads. Many questions were coming up. Being a diverse group that had just fought together defeating a determined and dangerous foe, there were many that questioned some of their traditions. Different groups had different traditions that had evolved over time. The prairie people's men established manhood by the taking of a buffalo and proving that they could be a valuable warrior in battle. The lake people had established a tradition that to be a man, one had to prove that he had the skills to provide for a family. Some young men had proven themselves in battle against the Redface. Some of the women had been fearless in battle, feeling themselves equal to any man. They accepted as their shaman a woman; she was the only one who had the skills and knowledge necessary.

Their evening fires became council meetings, not that they were declared a council meeting, but the discussions were the issues discussed at council. Snow was unanimously declared their chief. He had no say. Eventually, he resigned himself to his fate. Show had attended a variety of council meetings. He realized that the best leaders were the ones that said little and listened to the people. He did use his authority to try to give everyone a voice; giving everyone a chance to speak, insisting that all be given due respect. The women seemed to stand as a group, and the men wanted to retain their traditional roles. After several heated debates where Snow just listened, he stood and spoke.

"Are we to be one people that work together for the benefit of all? Or two groups, men and women, who coexist out of necessity in an adversarial manner?"

There was a long pause that made Snow wonder if he had spoken wrongly. Would the men think he was siding with the women? Would the women think he was patronizing them?

One of the women said, "You are the chief. Tell us what is right."

"I am your chief because you asked me to be the chief. A good chief listen to his people then leads in the direction that the people want. I will listen to all, then do my best."

Little Rose stood. "I stand with my husband, Snow."

It was late; time to get some rest. Everyone wanted to think about what Snow had said. He rarely spoke physiologically.

By midafternoon, they reached the little bear's mouth. The flow of water was too great to gain access to the valley beyond. A few jumped into one of the pools of water soon joined by many. The spring river water was cold; it was not long till everyone was out of the pool. They made camp some ways down the trail to get away from the water torrent's spray and mist. Fires were built to warm the flesh and to dry the clothing after the spontaneous celebration of life.

After the shelters were set up and bellies filled, the people gathered about one bonfire. Conversation started with the day's events. A herd of buffalo was seen way out upon the prairie. The prairie chickens tasted wonderful, which many tasted from the few that were harvested. There were some difficulties traveling the game trail they were following. Enthusiasm was high to see their new home in a couple of days.

When there was a pause in the conversation, a young man stood, saying, "I am Big Beaver from the Lake Village. Two springs ago, I came to the River Village as a rock thrower. I fought in two battles. I trained as a spear-thrower. Last spring, I went to the Red Rock Village, fighting in another battle. We are all from different tribes with different traditions. Red Bird, from the Village of Falling Waters, and I would like to bond together. We would like our bonding to be recognized by our new tribe. What are our traditions now?"

A young woman stood up and said, "I am Red Bird from the Village of Falling Waters. I chose to bond with Big Beaver."

This brought up many questions. Though they were all cousins, they were from different villages and different tribes with different traditions and rituals. They all did share the same virtues and values. Were they to become a new tribe? With what traditions, and what would they call themselves? The immediate question was how would they recognize and accept the bonding of Big Beaver and Red Bird?

Blue Bird, Little Rose's mother, a highly respected elder, stood up, saying, "Big Beaver and Red Bird have, respectively, asked us to approve their bonding. Big Beaver and Red Bird are respected assets to our people, the people of Big Bear Valley. I say that we accept them as a bonded man and woman in a ceremony of their choosing. Does anyone question this?"

There were many "Uhs" and no opposition.

No opposition to Blue Bird's statement resolved several questions. They were a tribe unto themselves, calling themselves the people of Big Bear Valley. Decisions affecting the tribe would be made by all in the tribe. A tradition for the bonding of a man and woman was established. Traditions would be established as necessary, taking the best of each tribe that all could agree upon.

It took four days for all to reach the Big Bear Valley and move all their possessions to a selected site for a village. By fall they had built lodges. They had found a supply of flint and salt. Life again became peaceful where the people could live in harmony within their world with an abundance of all they needed.

In time, news was brought that the Redface had made so many enemies, both from other tribes and from within, that they ceased to be.

Snow and Little Rose spent a lot of their time fishing, hunting, and exploring their new world. Their time together was what they relished. They tried to avoid the accolades given them. They encouraged the people to make the decisions affecting all. Neither desired power or authority. They had seen many die and be wounded under their orders. They did not want to be responsible for any more loss.

The Big Bear Valley proved to be much larger than they imagined. A five-day walk did not reveal the end of the valley to the east.

The people prospered. There were many births; many people of other villages joined the people of the Big Bear Valley. Setting Owl contrived a mechanism that used the river's current to dip nets into the water, providing a bounty of fish. Land was cleared where grain, roots, berries, and herbs were planted, providing all the food needed by the people.

Little Rose never gave birth to a child. She pleaded with Snow to take a second wife to bear him a child.

Snow told Little Rose, "You bring me such joy that I chose to not be with another woman. You make my life full."

As time passed, Snow and Little Rose decided to explore all their valley, not wanting to become complacent becoming fat and old. They wanted to share their time together doing what the enjoyed. They snuck off one morning, telling a few of their plans not wanting the attention they knew it would bring.

Snow and Little Rose never returned leaving a legend that was retold for many generations. They became revered as the founding father and mother of the People of the Big Bear Valley.

The Legend of Snow and Little Rose lives
on in the heart's of their people.

ABOUT THE AUTHOR

The author, D. C. Townsend, is retired and lives on a secluded ridge in the Northern Black Hills of South Dakota. Deer, elk, coyotes, turkey, rabbits, and squirrels, with an occasional eagle keep the author entertained between putting words on paper. The only thing that soars higher than the eagle, runs faster than a deer, or scurries up a tree more agilely than a squirrel, is the authors imagination. The author lives in a world of uninhibited imagination. There is also Buddy, a dog, who is almost as eccentric as his roommate. Buddy is a good listener, especially if being petted or awaiting dinner.

CPSIA information can be obtained
at www.ICGtesting.com
Printed in the USA
LVHW081037160422
716314LV00005B/219

9 781957 776040